Your

-A Novel Written by-
KC Blaze

Copyright © 2014 by True Glory Publications
Published by True Glory Publications LLC

www.urbanfictionnews.com

platinumfiction@yahoo.com

Twitter: @26kessa
This novel is a work of fiction. Any resemblances to actual events, real people, living or dead, organizations, establishments or locales are products of the author's imagination. Other names, characters, places, and incidents are used fictitiously.

Cover Design: Michael Horne
Editor: Kylar Bradshaw

All rights reserved. No part of this book may be used or reproduced in any form or by any means electronic or mechanical, including photocopying, recording or by information storage and retrieval system, without the written permission from the publisher and writer.

Because of the dynamic nature of the Internet, any Web addresses or links contained in this book may have changed since publication, and may no longer be valid. The views expressed in this work are solely those of the author and do not necessarily reflect the views of the publisher and the publisher hereby disclaims any responsibility for them.

Table of Contents

Acknowledgements………………………………....5
Suffer the Consequences………………..………6
When the Smoke Clears…..………………………13
Do the Right Thing……..……………….........20
Behind Bars………………………….…………31
Past Tense……………….……………………35
Two Steps Back……………………...…………44
When the Heart Hurts..…………….................52
*   Abandonment Hurts…………………….....59*
Time to Face Reality…………………………70
Thrown through a Loop…………………….78
Nowhere Else to Turn.………………………....82
Stranger than Reality…………..……………93
Unlikely Circumstances..…………………….99
Where Do I Go From Here?.............…………108
Put Your Mouth Where Your Mouth Is……….122
Decisions Decisions..…………………………..138
The Devils' Playground…………………….155
The Waiting Game……………………….164
Sign from God?........………………………....174
I Pay? No You Pay!...…………………………181
An Almost Perfect Night…………………….190
Time to Let Go………………………………204
Picking Sides……………………………...212
Lay It All on the Table……………………….221
Mind Made Up……………………………...232
Desperate Times Calls for Desperate Measures..245
Laughs Last………………………………….257

Your Husband, My Man
Part 2

By: K.C Blaze

Acknowledgments

I want to thank my family for engaging in my love of writing. For asking questions and telling me when I needed to improve something. I love you all and really appreciate you. I would also like to thank the readers of my work. I value your time, your reviews, feedback, and interest in my work. I seek to make you happy with characters you can relate to, obsess over, and gossip about. For as long as you take the time to read, I will take the time to create. God Bless!!!

Suffer the Consequences
Misha

I sat on the couch in what used to be my home looking dazed. I learned last night that my husband Tori was screwing my best friend Lauren for God knows how long. Though he carried me here expecting to talk, I no longer had anything to say. I was tired but I refused to sleep in the same house as his trifling ass. I looked over at him, slumped on the couch beside me sleeping. A big part of me wants to scratch his eyes out, beat him in his sleep, but I only stood up from the couch and walked toward the door. I finally saw clear enough to give him his divorce. I was a lot of things, but the one thing I have always been to him was loyal and faithful. He could have Lauren's selfish, gold digging ass; but when I was done with him, he would no longer have anything for her to take.

He didn't hear me leave out, which was good cause I was capable of just about anything at the moment. I reached into my bra and pulled out my cellphone. There were over thirty missed calls from my brother and my mom. I called into my voicemail to hear the messages first. My brother Jerry was probably pissed that I didn't bring his car back last night like I promised. My mother's voice came through first. She sounded worried.

"Misha baby, where are you? The police are looking for you. They came to the house saying they have a few questions. Please call me when you get this message to let me know you're ok." She hung up and the next message was from my brother Jerry.

"Misha, what the fuck did you do? The cops are looking for you and I swear if you did something illegal in my car I'm going to hurt you." He ended the message on that note.

I clicked the phone off. Police? I knew what I did was wrong, breaking into Lauren's house last night, but I didn't think she would call the cops on me. I ran back into the house and shook Tori awake. He batted his eyes and stretched a few times before sitting up. When he saw me standing in front of him, he began talking.

"Misha, look I'm sorry."

"Shut up Tori and listen. The police are looking for me," I yelled at him.

"What? The police? Who told you that?" he asked confused.

"My mom and brother left me a message saying the cops were there last night asking them questions. They were looking for me." I tried not to panic, but knowing the police were involved made me uneasy.

"I know you don't want to hear this, but I need to call Lauren." Tori's eyes apologized, but he was right. I needed to know how much damage my ex-best friend did.

"Fine." I flopped on the couch and flipped on the television. I would need to do something to keep me distracted or I would have a nervous breakdown.

The image of a young, pretty news anchor standing in front of a familiar building roped off with yellow tape appeared on the screen. The words Club Seduction set on fire crossed the screen and my heart dropped. Tori held his cell phone to his ear but looked in the direction of the TV. He ended the call with his mouth open.

"Oh shit, is that her club?" he asked. I couldn't speak, only nodded my head.

"Her phone is turned off. Did they say why they were looking for you?" His question was rhetorical because we both knew why. The pretty brunette informed us that the club owner was inside of the building when it caught on fire. My heart sank, I hoped they didn't think I had anything to do with this.

"Oh my God is she dead?" I asked aloud. We both sat in silence before I said, "I have to go the police station." I couldn't believe what was happening.

"Damn, you're right," Tori chimed in. I called my mom before I jumped up from the couch. She answered on the second ring.

"Misha?" her voice was panicked.

"Yes, I got your message. I think I'm in trouble." Were the only words that I could think to say.

"What did you do?" I knew she was crying, which pierced my heart.

"Mom, please don't cry. I'm fine, I will explain it to you later. I'm going over to the police station." I let her know my plan.

"I'll meet you there ok?" she yelled into the receiver before I hung up. I would have to go clear up the fact that I was responsible for hopping her fence and going into her condo, but that was it.

"I'll take you." Tori reached for his sneakers.

Despite the fact that I hated his guts at the moment, I didn't have any money for a taxi and my brother's car was parked a block away from Lauren's condo. I didn't speak to Tori, only walked outside and stood by the passenger side door. He unlocked the car with his keys, so I could get in. When he jumped in the driver side, he stared at me for a long moment.

"Mish, I really am sorry. I didn't want to hurt you like this." His lips were moving, but I tuned him out. I could only see images of Lauren riding him when I walked into her bedroom. I didn't respond to his apology, which forced him to turn on the car and back out of the driveway. I looked cool as ice on the outside, but my heart was threatening to beat out of my chest. I should have listened to my brother last night and just stayed home after we left the club.

When Tori pulled up to the police station my strong persona fell by the way side and I began to cry. He tried to hug me, but I shrugged his arms off of me.

"Don't touch me, you should probably go see if your girlfriend is still alive," I snapped. I jumped out of his car at the same moment my mom flew out of a taxi. Soon as she saw me, she hugged me tight. Tori stepped out of the Challenger and stood behind me. My mom looked at him sideways, but kept hugging me. I sent up a prayer, *God please get me out of this.* With that I inhaled deeply, pulled my shoulders back and walked the stairs of the police station with my soon to be ex-husband and my overly emotional mother following closely behind.

When the Smoke Clears
Lauren

My eyes felt dry as I tried to open them under the bright lights of the hospital room. The last thing I remember is being surrounded by smoke as I was locked inside of my club. I could hear the sound of my father's voice talking in the background. When my eyes finally focused, I looked around the small emergency room. I was hooked up to an oxygen mask with tubes coming from my arms connecting me to monitors. My dad walked over to the bed.

"Lauren honey," I turned to look at him. He looked like he hasn't slept in days. My throat was dry and it hurt to swallow.

"Don't talk, just know that I'm here. I let the police know about your incident with Misha earlier and they're going to investigate it ok?" I nodded my head yes, but I couldn't really believe Misha would go this far. I knew she was crazy when she was angry and she did pull a knife on me and Tori, but I can't say that I actually blame her under the circumstances. I was happy to be alive and then I remembered my club.

"Dad? My club." My voice came out raspy

"Don't worry honey, your insurance will cover most of the damage. The fire department was able to stop the fire before it did any major damage." He tried to calm my nerves, but I was devastated. I just launched the commercials to get more exposure and would have to close to renovate.

"My car?" The words forced themselves from my lips.

"Lauren, stop worrying honey. I'm happy you made it out alive. You can get a new car." A new car? My car was custom made, I loved my car.

"What happened to my car daddy?" Tears welled in my eyes. I couldn't believe all of this shit was happening to me all at once.

"Your car was set on fire, it is completely totaled honey, now get some rest ok? I'll be out here in the waiting room with Shannon." He kissed me on the forehead before stepping out into the hall way.

If Misha really wanted to hurt me, she knew how to do it. She ruined my club and my car. I wanted to ask my dad did anyone else come to see me, but he already left. I never felt so alone in my life. I wondered how long I was knocked out, how long I had been in the hospital. Some of my questions would soon be answered with the awkward young male doctor coming into my room.

"Ms. Michaels? How you feeling?" he asked like he expected me to say I felt great. I just sat in silence until he started talking again.

"Right now you're in stable condition. We are going to keep you here for another night for observation. You're lucky the police came in time." He patted my knee before checking my IV fluid and the monitors. "A nurse will be here shortly to check your vital signs ok? For now try to get some rest." Just like that he was gone. I couldn't take this anymore. I needed to hear from Tori, I needed to know that he was still my man. I needed to know that he cared about me, but most importantly that he was still leaving Misha.

The thought of me going through all of this for nothing was too much to think about, so I closed my eyes and took a deep breath. The image of my mother flashed before me. I hadn't thought about her in years. The image came in crystal clear, it was the same day my dad took me out of the house. My mom was still beautiful even with tears staining her honey colored face. She was screaming, begging my dad not to take me. I could see a man sitting on the couch. He looked familiar, but I couldn't make out his face. I heard him saying sorry repeatedly. The last image was of five year old me being escorted out of the house by my father. He cursed my mother and pushed her until she fell on the floor before my memory faded. I didn't know why that memory resurfaced. I knew my mom cheated on my dad and that's why he left her that was really all I knew about her. He never wanted to talk about my mom and kept me preoccupied with life lessons and gifts to divert my attention.

As soon as I hit puberty and my boobs began to grow, my dad started giving me little speeches about the birds and the bees. He told me that men were only as good as their word. He would say if a man promise you the world make him give you the moon as a down payment. I used to think he was partially insane, but I soon saw what he meant. During high school I had plenty of boys saying just about everything to get into my panties. So while all of the other girls were giving it up for ten dollar earrings and a chance to wear a varsity jacket, I was demanding the real thing. I learned that men were capable of telling you anything to get what they wanted so I would benefit from the transaction.

I was well trained in catching bull shit and could spot a hustle from ten miles away. I learned the art of manipulation so well I became a master of the game. However, it was something about Tori that I had to have. I never expected to want anyone for no reason other than love. He makes me feel like I can have everything and here he is wasting it all on Misha. My thoughts were abruptly interrupted by a loud knock on the door. Seconds later two uniformed policemen came walking in with my father close behind.

"Ms. Michaels, we have a few questions for you if you're up to it." The shorter of the two stated. I reached for the paper cup filled with ice to wet my throat. My dad walked by the police officers to get the cup and put it to my mouth.

Do the Right Thing
Tori

Seeing Lauren's club on the morning news made me want to panic. I hoped she was alright, but my first reaction was to make sure Misha didn't get in trouble for it. When we walked into the police station a detective took her into a room to get her side of the story. She was in there for what felt like ages. It wasn't long before a chubby red haired cop escorted me into a room with a table and two chairs. I felt like I was on an episode of Law & Order, but this wasn't scripted.

"Have a seat. Mr. Carter, is it?" he asked with a slight Irish accent.

"I'm Officer Delaney. I have a few questions for you," he continued as I took a seat at the table. Sweat formed around my collar.

"We have Misha Carter in another room and just need to cross check her story. Who is Misha Carter to you?" he asked, though he already knew.

"She's my wife." I folded my hands to keep from moving them around while I spoke.

"Your wife, ok. We have a report from 1:30 am stating Mrs. Carter trespassed at a Lauren Michaels' residence is that correct?" his question wasn't a clear cut yes or no question, but he tried to make it that way.

"Misha did come to Lauren's house," I started, but he quickly cut me off.

"She was there uninvited?" he asked again.

"It's not that simple. Misha and I were thinking about getting a divorce because of a previous issue. I was seeing her best friend Lauren," I hesitated. I knew it would sound bad if I told the truth.

"You were having an affair with her best friend?" He started writing on a small notepad. It made me more nervous.

"Yes, ok and then what?" I started thinking about the fire at the night club and I began to suspect they were trying to pin this on Misha, but she was with me.

"Look, Misha walked in on us having sex. She was upset and tried to explain herself on the previous issue," I kept going.

"The report says there was a knife involved." He tried to give me a nonchalant, just doing my job look, but I knew what police did to unprepared black people. I had to tread lightly or Misha would be in a world of trouble.

"She came in with a knife, but she didn't try to hurt us. She only came in talking. She was crying and just said she was going to give me my divorce. Lauren threw something at her and attacked her and the knife sliced across her face. Misha didn't intentionally stab her or hurt her. I convinced Misha to leave with me and I drove us back to my house. We fell asleep together on the couch." I studied his face. I wasn't able to read if he believed me or not.

"So she was with you between the hours of 3am to 5am?" Officer Delaney asked while still jotting things down on his notepad.

"Yes, she was."

"Are you aware that Ms. Michaels' club was set on fire?" he asked staring intently on me now.

"Yes, we saw it on the news right before we came here," I answered honestly.

"Have you tried to contact Ms. Michael's after you left her residence?" he asked with a serious face.

"I tried calling her this morning until I saw the news. Her phone was turned off, it went straight to voicemail." He stood up from the table and walked out of the room. I took a deep breath and waited for him to return.

I was scared, but I told the truth so we should be fine. A few minutes later he came back in the room.

"You're free to go. If we have any more questions or if you recall anything else, here's my card." I took the card and put it in my pants pocket. When I walked out of the small room, I expected to see Misha and her mom waiting for me instead it was just her mom. Her eyes were wide with fear and she was mumbling prayers. Within a few minutes Misha was being escorted out of a room in handcuffs, my heart dropped. Why was she still being arrested? She had tears running down her face and her head low.

"Hold on officer. Why is she being arrested?" I walked up to one of the policemen holding her by the arm.

"Criminal trespassing and assault and battery." I couldn't believe this. My mother in law fell into me and I grabbed her quickly to hold her up. This was all my fault.

"Misha don't worry about this ok? I'm going to get you out within a few hours," I spoke to her, but she only stared at me with sad eyes. I did this to my family and I don't think I would be able to forgive myself.

"I'm going to get you out ok?" I kept talking to her until I couldn't see her anymore.

"Come on." I held on to my mother in law and walked her back out of the building.

"What's going to happen to her?" she asked and I wanted to answer, but I really didn't know.

"I'm not sure mom, but I'm going to get her out. I promise." I held the car door open so she could get in.

It was time for me to see Lauren. I needed to know what happened. I dropped my mother in law off at her house and drove back to my house to shower and change. On my way into the bathroom, I dialed Lauren's number again, but it went to voicemail. My next thought was to google the nearest hospital to her night club. I got the number and called the emergency room.

"Hello, I'm checking to see if a Lauren Michaels was admitted to the hospital this morning?" I asked calmly.

"Hold on while I check." The female nurse spoke into the receiver. Elevator music filled my ear until she came back.

"Yes, she is here." She gave me the information. I thanked her before hanging up and taking my shower.

On the ride over to the hospital I kept picturing what I would say, hoping no one else was there and I tried to prepare for what I might see. When I got there, I was given her room number by a petite blond nurse. I followed the numbers until I reached room 13. I knocked once before opening the door. She was there alone, which was nice. Her eyes remained closed, unlike my vivid imagination she looked normal. She opened her eyes and smiled when she saw me.

"Tori." Her voice came in raspy and hushed, but I could tell she was happy to see me.

"Hey," I pulled up a chair. A wave of mixed emotions flooded me. I felt bad seeing Lauren connected to machines, but guilt replaced attraction. She reached out to touch my hand. I took it in mine briefly before setting it back in her lap.

"Are you ok?" I asked with real concern.

"I'm fine, they're keeping me here for observation. I'm so happy you came." She tried to turn her body in my direction.

"Did you call the cops on Misha last night?" There was no other way for me to ask her without it sounding insensitive. But my wife was in jail and I needed to move fast. I could see the irritation in the back of her eyes, but I couldn't care about that right now.

"I did call the cops cause her ass was out of line." She elevated her voice for a second.

"Lauren, you know she wasn't going to hurt us. She was upset about catching us," I said. I was trying to reason with her not make her upset.

"Tori, she had a knife. She was going to do more than hurt us and she tried to burn my ass to death," she said between coughs.

"Lauren, Misha was with me last night. I took her back to my house and we didn't leave there until this morning. She didn't go back to your club. They arrested her, but I'm telling you she didn't try to kill you last night." I studied her face for a sign, instead she turned her face away from me.

"You only came here to talk about Misha?" she asked above a whisper.

"She's in trouble and a big part of it is my fault. I'm not going to let her sit in jail for something I know she didn't do." I was getting irritated with Lauren. She wanted to make things about me and her when the reality is we shouldn't have been seeing each other from the start.

"Tori, I thought you came here to check on me. You're divorcing Misha remember? So why do you care what the fuck happens to her? I'm your woman or don't you remember that anymore?" she had tears running down her face and I asked myself when did things get so complicated.

"Lauren, you're a good woman, but Misha is my wife. Until she's out and all of this goes away, I can't focus on anything else." I had to keep it real. I wasn't going to be acting like her man when my heart told me that I needed to fix my marriage with Misha.

Lauren turned her back on me. I didn't have anything else to say so I stood up and walked out of the hospital room. I would need to find out if they were going to let Misha out on bail. I drove out of the hospital parking lot and headed over to the police station. I fucked up worse than anything Misha has ever done to me. I remembered seeing her face on our wedding day. She looked beyond happy, I could see love in her eyes. Now all I saw was disgust and vowed to change that.

Behind Bars
Misha

I heard Tori's words about getting me out, but I no longer believed in his abilities. I was looking at the man I called husband for over eight years, but I couldn't recognize him anymore. A detective asked me a few questions in a small, stuffy room in the back of the police station. I told them the truth. I told them how I climbed over the gate, how I saw Tori and Lauren having sex, and how I walked into her house with the intention of confronting them both. I confessed to grabbing a knife out of the kitchen and going into her bedroom. I told them I wasn't sure of what I planned on doing, but I knew I wanted Tori to hear me out about the adoption situation. They started asking me where I was during the time of the fire and I let them know I was with Tori though I wished I wasn't.

They informed me that I was under arrest for criminal trespassing and assault and battery because of the knife cutting Lauren's face and arm. I wanted to be cool, but I started crying when I saw my mom. Tori actually looked scared, but it was because of his cheating ass that I was in this trouble to start with. Sitting in this cold cell with a group of four other women made me realize how quickly your life can take a turn. I fixed my face to read, Try a bitch, so the other chicks in there wouldn't test me. There was only one chick in here spazing out. I couldn't believe I was fingerprinted and booked. I took a moment to think over everything and I guessed it made sense for Lauren to come after Tori. He was fine as hell, built like a brick wall, and smart. Most importantly, he was married. I knew she only went after married dudes but she usually only wanted men who had lots of money, way more money than Tori.

Though I didn't set her club on fire I knew who ever did was tired of her shit too. I had to trust that God wouldn't let me pay for the fire. I was willing to pay the consequences for what I actually did do even though she attacked me and cut her own damn self. She lucky that's all that happened. If Tori didn't stop me, I probably would have stabbed her ass to death. I forced myself to think about something else cause I didn't want to cry thinking about Tori fucking Lauren. If her ass wasn't already dead I planned on choking her the fuck out the first minute I got.

"What you in for?" A dark skinned woman with dreads scooted over a few spaces on the dirty bench beside me. She wanted to strike up a conversation or probe for information to help her with her own case.

"For minding my damn business, now back the fuck up," I said rudely. I didn't need friends and though this was my first actual arrest I grew up in the hood so this shit wasn't new to me.

"Damn bitch, you ain't have to get smart." She moved back to her original spot.

"But I did. Keep your ass over there and I will keep mine over here." I rolled my eyes to add emphasis to my statement. I didn't have time to be making friends with none of this broads.

I was getting restless, they had me here for at least four hours already and no word on what was going on. I only hoped Tori was really trying his best to get me out.

Past Tense
Lauren

I couldn't believe Tori would come up to the hospital and talk to me about Misha. He didn't ask if I was ok or if I needed anything. I don't like losing, so I will do whatever it takes to make him want me again. I was better than Misha's ghetto ass and Tori knew it. So, if it meant dropping the charges on Misha, I would. However, I was going to make sure her ass paid for the fire. I looked at the clock on the wall of the hospital. It was just about time for my dad to arrive. I know things are strained between him and Shannon right now but her ass needs to get over it.

I reached for my cell and turned it on. There were over seventy text messages and a ton of voicemails. I noticed that Chris reached out to me a few times. I decided to give him a call first. I used the hospital phone by the bed and dialed his number.

"Chris? It's Lauren," I stated when he answered.

"Damn girl. What the fuck happened to you? I saw what happened to the club on the news." He seemed worried.

"I know. I'm in the hospital, but I'm doing better. Somebody tried to kill my ass." I paused to think about that for a second.

"Damn, that's fucked up. What you need me to do?" he asked.

"I need you to tell everybody that the club is going to be down for a few weeks. I'm still paying everybody regular salary while its down. I need you to call the insurance company, so they can assess the damage and we can have the work done. I can't have this shit messing with my investor's money." I spit out orders for Chris to start making power moves before I hung up.

My dad entered the room a few seconds later, he was by himself. I guess Shannon didn't want to look the woman who was screwing her brother in law in the face.

"Hey daddy." He kissed me on the forehead.

"Hey baby girl, how you feeling?" he asked before taking a seat.

"I feel a bit better. I just told Chris to start calling the insurance company. Where's Shannon?" I really didn't care where she was, but needed to hear him tell me.

"She decided to stay at home today. Don't worry about her, ok? So is Chris going to handle everything?" he changed the subject.

"Tell me the truth dad, she doesn't want to look me in the face?" I wasn't going to let it go easily. I was tired of him handling me with kid gloves. There was a huge elephant in the room and I was prepared to address it.

"No, she didn't. She's upset that you would be so reckless." Reckless? I was being reckless or was Arnold?

"Reckless?" I asked with pure indignation in the back of my words.

"You were dating a married man, not just any married man, but her brother in law. So yes, she feels you were reckless." My father has never talked to me this way before like he was disgusted by me.

"I know what I did was wrong, but he was just as guilty daddy. You always told me to never hustle backwards, so I don't. You think I was with him for love? Everything Club Seduction has become is because of the work I put in with Arnold," I screamed at him.

"Screwing a married man is not putting in work Lauren." He stood up and stormed out of the room. His words cut deeper than any knife.

I could hear him talking low to someone on the outside of the door. The words weren't clear and then a brief knock against the door made me turn my face to see a woman rush in with my father trailing close behind. I couldn't believe I was staring at an older version of the woman I carried around in my wallet. My mother stood wide eyed in the hospital doorway. My father reaching for her arm to pull her out of the room.

"Let her go," I yelled at my father.

"Lauren," he spoke.

"I said let her go dad." He pushed her arm and walked angrily out of the room. She didn't move for a few minutes only stared at me.

"Oh wow, you're so grown up." She finally spoke. Words caught in my throat. I didn't know what to say to the woman who gave me life, but didn't care enough to raise me.

"That's what kids do they grow up," I answered. I couldn't take my eyes off of her. She was thinner now than in the picture, her hair was wavy, and hung around her shoulders. Her brown eyes were still beautiful.

"Can I sit down?" she asked nervously like she expected me to throw her out of the room.

"Sure why not." I didn't mean to be rude, but she was a mystery, only a woman I use to know.

"I heard about what happened on the news," she started.

"One shot at my fifteen minutes of fame and it's about me trapped in a burning building." She smiled at my attempt at humor.

"I had a lot of things I planned to say, but right now I'm drawing a blank." She played with a napkin in her hands.

"Well, we can start with the fact that you waited all of these years to reach out to me." I looked her dead in the eye. She put her head down.

"I tried reaching out to you, but your father moved around and never gave me your address. I spoke with him once and he told me it would be better if you thought I was dead." The words came out of her mouth and made both our eyes well with tears. Why the fuck would my dad think that would be better.

"What did you do to make him hate you so much?" I wanted an answer and today I was going to get it.

"Your father is not the man you think he is." She started wiping away tears with her now shredded napkin. What did she mean he wasn't the man I thought I knew? Who was she to talk trash about him? She was the one who stepped out on the relationship.

"You cheated on him, so how you gonna come in here talking trash about my dad," I elevated my voice. A few seconds later my dad opened the room door and walked up to my mother.

"It's time to go." He grabbed her arm forcefully and started dragging her out of the room.

"You have to believe me. Find me at the Church, Christian Fellowship. Lauren, please find me at the church!" she was screaming while my dad pulled her out of the room. He tried to cover her mouth, but she kept screaming until a group of nurses came to check in on me.

My dad stuck around until they finally discharged me and gave me a lift back over to my condo. He insisted on checking out the entire house before he felt comfortable enough to leave. I didn't ask him what my mother meant, I knew he wouldn't tell me the truth. He did however, ask me several times what she said. I made something up and repeated it each time. It felt bittersweet to be back at my place. The last time I was here I was making love to Tori and rudely interrupted by my ex-best friend Misha. It was painful knowing my Jaguar was blown to smithereens. If what Tori said was true about Misha being with him, however irritating it was it made me think about who was trying to blow up my damn club with me in it.

I put my phone on the charger and sent Arnold a text telling him where I was. He didn't answer for a half hour.

It was Sunday so I knew he was home with his wife. I wasn't interested in keeping things going with Arnold, but I needed his legal advice and I knew his buddies would want to hear my plans for the club, especially with their money invested in it. Chris sent me a text telling me that he reached out to the claims department of my insurance company. They would send someone out tomorrow morning to evaluate the damage. I thanked him and headed to the bathroom. I desperately needed a bubble bath. I sent Tori a text asking him if we could talk. I needed him more than anything to make me feel somewhat safe.

Two Steps Back
Tori

I was finally able to get Misha out with a fifteen hundred dollar bail. I was waiting for her to walk through the doors of the precinct when the text from Lauren came through. I deleted the message without reading it. Misha came strutting out of the doors like she's seen more in those few hours than in her entire lifetime. I stood up to hug her, but she pushed passed me and walked out the front doors.

"Mish," I started, but she cut me off immediately.

"Look, don't think shit's changed alright. I saw your trifling ass fucking my best friend. She can keep your ass if she wants you cause I'm still done," she snapped out on me in front of the police station. I forgot how good she looked when she's angry.

"I know you're mad, but I want to talk to you." I walked behind her.

"I'm not mad muthafucka, I'm just done. Are you taking me home or am I taking a cab." She looked at me with pure venom so I unlocked the car doors. She sat down in the passenger seat before I could open the door for her. I jogged around to the driver side.

"You want to talk to me now? I've been calling your ass for damn near a month and you've ignored me and now you have something to say." She clicked her seatbelt, laughed like she was insane, and pulled her hair out of her face.

I knew there was really nothing I could say, but I was determined to keep my wife. I started driving to my house.

"Where are you going? My mom's house is that way." She pointed behind her.

"I'm taking you home," I said without looking her way.

"The same home you kicked me out of? You must have lost your damn mind. Open the door. Open the fucking door, Tori. Your ass is obviously insane!" she started screaming at me. I didn't care what she said, I planned on taking her home to reason with her.

"If you don't open the damn doors and let me out I swear I'm going to get every last damn one of my brothers to kick your ass," she threatened.

"Misha, shut up with that. We both know your brothers can't fight worth shit," I snapped at her.

"We'll see, you think I'm going to tolerate your cheating ass? I don't think so. I hope you're enjoying the last few rides in my car cause I'm taking it too," she continued her rant.

I turned off at my exit and maneuvered through the streets until I pulled into my parking lot.

"I'm not getting out so your ass better start the damn car and take me to my mother's house." I opened my door, walked around to her side of the car. She was still talking shit inside. I opened her door and reached in to undo her seatbelt. She started pushing me away, but I was stronger.

"I'm not going any fucking where." She tried to cross her arms, but I picked her up out of the car, threw her over my shoulder, and walked toward the house.

"Put me the fuck down, cheating ass liar." I used my key to get in with her hitting me in the back. I knew a few of my neighbors were watching, but they were already used to our fights.

I sat her on the couch before I closed the front door. I needed to calm the lady killer cause he was turned on by all of the commotion.

"I know you want to leave and I will let you, but I think we should talk first. If you let me speak my peace, I will let you go if you want to leave." I knew I wasn't being fair, but I wasn't willing to let her walk out the door that easily, blame it on the male ego.

Misha didn't say anything only twisted her lips and crossed her arms. I knew she would at least let me talk. Now, I just needed to figure out what I wanted to say.

"I know the shit is foul, but I didn't start fucking around with Lauren cause I didn't love you. When I first got this job, I thought you were going to celebrate with me at her club, but you changed your mind. That night she treated me like a fucking king. She roped off VIP, kept the alcohol flowing, and I helped her clean up. I'm not sure what happened, but we kissed and the rest is history. I have no excuse for what I did, but Mish you have to meet me half way. You were being mean as hell all the time. You pushed me away, made me feel like shit, and you made me feel wrong for wanting to make love to my wife." I waited for an answer, but she sat in silence with tears streaming down her face, so I kept talking.

"I thought you didn't want me anymore and that's how I justified it. When I saw that adoption letter in your bag, I was pissed as hell cause I thought you hated me enough to get rid of my seed. I didn't know you did what you did to save me from being like my deadbeat ass father. I don't want to lose you, Mish, and I'm willing to do whatever it takes to get you back. I'm not going anywhere." By the end of my speech I was sitting on the floor beside her legs. When I didn't say anything else I felt Misha stand up. She walked directly in front of me and stopped.

"Now, I let you get everything off your chest, but I want you to know one thing. I loved you all the way up until I saw you through the window of my best friend's house. I would have begged and pleaded forever to be back in your good graces, but now I realize something. I realize that I have protected you from your greatest fears our entire relationship. I placed my damn child up for ADOPTION for you. I'm done with you, this marriage, and everything it stood for. You deserve Lauren, a lying, gold digging ass bitch, who sucks her man dry by giving him an illusion of what he thinks he wants. You wanted a knock off when you've had the real deal. So fuck you Tori and the next time you see me it will be in divorce court." She walked out the front door leaving me paralyzed. I wanted to run after her, but I felt the weight of her words holding me in place.

I didn't move from my spot on the floor until the moon replaced the sun and both my bladder and my hunger took over my senses. I ignored the ringing of my cell phone, the barrage of text messages pinging the entire time I sat there. The only thing I could think about was when I first met Misha. I was a slim sixteen year old kid. I saw her walking home from school one day and followed behind her whistling. She finally turned around, put her hand on her hip and said, 'I see you know how to whistle, but if you don't know how to talk please stop following me.' I laughed to myself. She was the only girl who spoke so bluntly. I didn't have a comeback, so I fell back. The next time I saw her she told me to get my weight up. I started doing pushups after that. We didn't start talking seriously until we turned eighteen. I was so damned happy she finally gave me a shot that I vowed to never blow it.

When the Heart Hurts
Misha

When I got in the house my mom jumped up from the table crying like she thought she'd never see me again. I made my brother pay the cab out front and told him where he could find his car. I made the cab driver ride pass to be sure it was still there. After things calmed down, I told my mom what happened. She looked just as disgusted as I did when I was there. She didn't tell me I was right, but she squeezed my hand and said she understood now. I was going to call a lawyer in the morning. For now I just wanted to jump in the shower and wash the stench of jail off my skin.

My cries were concealed by the running of the shower head. I gave Tori his chance to speak because I knew how being ignored can drive you to do some crazy shit. I only acted brave when I walked out of the house, but my heart felt like it could stop at any moment. I wished I was one of these chicks who could just forgive and forget, but the image of his betrayal would forever be etched in my mind. I let the warm water run over my body. I told myself to cry for the last time because the new Misha would arrive by morning. The two traitors would regret the day they decided to betray me.

After my shower I went into my new, old room and fell asleep curled up like a baby. It wasn't until the sun hit my face and the smell of pancakes and bacon woke me up the following morning. I knew what I needed to do today and I wouldn't stop until it was complete. I brushed my teeth and washed my face before joining my mother for breakfast. Jerry already left for work, so I wouldn't be able to get a ride from him. It would be ok though because while I was sitting in jail yesterday I remembered the credit card I had in my name. It was an emergency card that I didn't tell Tori about. With a ten thousand dollar limit I was going to use it wisely.

"Good morning mama." She looked confused by my cheerful disposition.

"How you feeling this morning?" she asked.

"Like a new woman. I'm going to find me a divorce lawyer today." I sat down right before she sat a plate of scrambled eggs, bacon and pancakes in front of me.

"Thank you mama." I smiled and began to eat.

Breakfast was filled with generic conversation. I wasn't telling anyone my plans, not even my well-meaning mother. After breakfast I slipped into one of my sexiest black dresses, put on my strappy stilettos and did my makeup like I planned to meet Obama. I called Enterprise rental car and had them send me a Nissan Altima I was renting for the next two weeks. As soon as the driver got there, I was out. I drove to downtown Atlanta until I reached the tall building I was looking for. I knew who I needed for this case and I would be sure he would be interested in what I had to say.

I walked into the office of Rosen, Marshal and Blake Law Firm with a mission. The pretty receptionist asked how she could help me and I asked to speak with Arnold Blake.

"Just a moment please." She directed me to a chair while she called to inform him he had a potentially new client.

"He'll be with you shortly," she stated before going back to her work. I sat patiently knowing that Mr. Blake would be floored to see me. As soon as Arnold walked out, he tensed briefly before putting on his best fake smile.

"Misha, how can I help you?" He nervously adjusted his suit jacket.

"I have a legal matter I want to discuss with you." I stood from my seat and headed in the direction of the office I saw him exit from. He followed closely behind and shut the door behind us both.

"Why are you here?" he asked through clenched teeth. I could have almost laughed.

"Because I have a pressing matter to discuss. I am pretty sure you'll want to hear it." I sat down in the chair in front of his desk, forcing him to take a seat or talk to my back.

"You tried to kill Lauren, I hope you're not here to ask me to represent you," he spoke with unresolved anger.

"For the record, I didn't try to kill Lauren, though it would have been understandable. I caught her and my husband fucking the night she was cut on her face. I didn't even lunge at her to cut her she threw something at me and attacked me." I studied his face. His jaw tightened, eyes silently searching for understanding, but he remained cool.

"What are you talking about?" he asked instead.

"You heard me right, Arnold. I saw you come to the club to see Lauren. I didn't know why she ushered you out so fast. I know why now. It was because my husband was there with her. I left the club early with my brother and then came back alone. I admit I followed Tori, but didn't know he was headed over to Lauren's. When I saw him drive through her security gate, I parked my car a block away and climbed the fence and there the two lying, backstabbing cheaters were fucking in her living room," I repressed my anger.

Arnold stood from his chair, though he was cheating on his wife with Lauren it hurt him to learn she was cheating on him. Men were such hypocritical bastards.

"What do you want me to do?" he finally asked after processing what I just told him.

"I want you to represent me in my divorce," I stated matter of factly.

"I'm a criminal attorney, Misha. I don't handle divorce cases." He looked at me with sad eyes.

"You do today. The best way to pay them both back is to use you for my divorce. I don't care what it will cost me. I want it done and I want it all." I wasn't leaving without him agreeing to represent me. I watched as he thought it over.

"I will represent you pro bono, give me a few hours to draw up the divorce papers, and to have him served." A smile wider than the Mississippi River spread across my face.

"Here's my number. Please call me when you serve him. I would love to be there to see his face." I passed Arnold a sheet of paper with both my cell phone number and my mother's number along with Tori's address.

"I would prefer to have you hold off on sharing the news with Lauren until after Tori has the divorce papers."

Thanks again." I stood to walk away.

"Misha?" Arnold called out to me.

"Yes."

"You look great." He gave me a compliment. I walked away smiling. Today was going to be a great day.

Abandonment Issues
Lauren

Tori never called me back and neither did Arnold. I was feeling like I needed to expand my network of friends. I decided to do a bold move, Chris drove me over to a car rental place so I could have something to ride around in. He was loyal to the end. With a sexy new silver BMW, I headed over to Tori's office. I thought I'd surprise him by inviting him to lunch. But I was to be surprised when I learned he took the day off. I sent him a quick text and would call if he didn't answer. I drove in the direction of his house, convincing myself that what I was doing was in the name of love. I just hoped he didn't have Misha there. I saw his car parked in the driveway, so I parked curbside and boldly walked up to the door and knocked.

My heart was beating a thousand miles a minute. If Misha was in the house, I was prepared to fight. There was no answer for a few minutes, so I knocked again. Then I saw the shades move. A second later I heard the door unlock. Tori opened it to say he wasn't himself would be an understatement.

"What?" he asked. His wife beater was dirty, he looked like he hadn't eaten, showered or shaved for days.

"What do you mean what? You don't answer your phone?" I asked partially irritated that he didn't let me in.

"Lauren, I'm not doing this ok? So leave." He tried to push the door close, but I pushed it open.

"Tori, what's going on? Talk to me please." I couldn't believe I was begging a man to talk to me. I was the solution to all of their relationship problems and he was starting to make me feel like I was the problem.

"There ain't shit to talk about Lauren. Misha wants the divorce," he said it like he was really devastated about it.

"Tori, you wanted the divorce first so what is the fucking problem?"

"I don't have to explain shit to you. Get the fuck away from my house. I don't want a divorce and I damn sure don't want to see your ass no more, so bounce!" he yelled at me before slamming the door. My heart dropped into my shoes.

I stood there for a few minutes, stunned at what just happened. After recouping I stumbled back to my car like I was hit with a bat. No one has ever talked to me like that before. I dropped to my car like there was a ton of bricks in my pockets. Tori wasn't thinking straight so I would give him a few days to get his shit together. I sat in the car feeling empty. I want Tori so bad, I want him to hold me. Right now everything is so shaky. Tears began to flow down my face and for a minute I felt like ramming his house with this pretty BMW. Then I remembered my mom. Her words screaming for me to find her at the church rang in my ears. I turned the ignition and pulled off.

There are a thousand churches in Atlanta, but I knew which church she was talking about. Instinctively, I remembered Christian Fellowship Church. I remember her taking me there on Sundays. I drove toward the church tired of feeling abandoned. I need closure and today I would get it from someone. The church was beautiful, a large green perfectly manicured lawn. Rose bushes covered the walkway. I parked and walked toward the front of the church. The doors were opened to my surprise. There was a receptionist in the front lobby.

"Hello sistah, how can I help you?" she asked.

"I'm looking for Diane Moore." I held my breath that was the first time in over fifteen years I actually said her name aloud.

"Oh sistah Diane, she just left. Can I let her know who asked for her?" the older woman answered. My mom works at the church.

"Her daughter," I said a little above a whisper.

"Lauren? Oh wait sweetie your mom told me to give you something." I was shocked that she knew my name. She started looking around for something on her desk. A second later she was handing me an envelope.

"Thank you." I reached for it and turned to leave.

"God is good, you look just like your mama," the receptionist said to my back. I didn't turn to comment only walked toward my car.

I hesitated briefly before ripping the top of the envelope. There was a piece of paper with nothing, but an address on it. I put the address in the car's GPS and let it guide me to the house on the paper. The robotic female voice let me know my destination was on the right fifteen minutes later. I parked behind a beaten up blue Chevy, grabbed the paper and my purse and got out of the car. There was nothing spectacular about the house. It was a one story townhome with a large tree in front. I knocked on the door and looked over my shoulder. Seconds later a tall brown skinned man with my father's face opened it. My heart caught in my throat.

"Yes?" he asked.

"I'm, I'm here for Diane Moore. It's Lauren," I forced the words out of my mouth. What type of joke was this? He stopped to stare at me for a few moments.

"Joe, who is it?" I heard my mother's voice behind him. He turned to face her.

"I'm sorry come in." Joe stepped aside for me to enter and my mom ran up and wrapped her arms around me tightly.

"Lauren, you came. She came Joe." She looked at the man with my father's face.

"Come in, come in. Sit down." She took me by the hand and led me to a flower print sofa in the living room. Pictures of me as a child lined the fireplace.

"Joe give us a minute, please." She looked over her shoulder to ask for privacy.

"Sure, you thirsty?" he directed his question to me.

"No, thank you." I was confused, who was he and why did he look like my damn father.

"What is this?" I asked for a lack of a better phrase.

"Thanks for coming Lauren, I'm really happy you came. I know you may want answers and I want to give them to you." Damn right, I wanted answers and I wanted them fast. I sat silent so she continued.

"Where do I start?" she asked herself.

"When I was twenty years old I met Joe, your father's brother. He was funny and gorgeous and kind. We fell in love almost instantly. When he introduced me to his family I was so, so excited. That's when I met your father. He was just as funny and charming, but he took my politeness for interest and began flirting with me. I admit I flirted with him a little more than I should, but I really thought it was harmless." She took a breath to examine my face. I was hearing what she was saying, but nothing registered.

"Ok?" I asked impatiently.

"One day I came over to your grandmother's house looking for Joe. Your dad answered and told me to come in. While I was in the living room he ran upstairs and then told me Joe said come up. When I got to Joe's room he wasn't there. Your dad pushed me into Joe's room and locked the door. I thought he was playing around, so I laughed it off and told him to let me out, but he wouldn't. He forced himself on me. I broke up with Joe, I couldn't bring myself to tell him what his brother did. A few weeks later I found out I was pregnant. I didn't know what to do, so I kept it to myself. One day I saw your dad, he saw my swollen belly and begged me to tell him what he already knew, that you were his. He begged me to let him be a part of your life. I didn't want you to grow up without your dad, so I agreed. It took me four years to build up enough courage to tell Joe what happened. He wanted to kill your father, but I talked him out of it. Me and Joe started seeing each other again and your dad came over one day unannounced. He came in acting a fool cause his brother's car was out front. That's the day he took you from me." When she stopped speaking, tears were making their way down my face.

I couldn't believe that my father would do that to someone. I refused to believe that he could rape anyone. What she was saying is that I was conceived out of rape.

"What are you telling me? What are you saying?" I asked in disbelief. "I remember that day and you were screaming sorry. I heard you saying sorry." I spoke through tears.

"That was you Lauren. You were apologizing to your dad to make him stop screaming."

"Why didn't you fight for me? Why didn't you fight to get me back?" I yelled at her. Joe now stood in the doorway.

"We didn't know where your father took you, he disappeared, and believe me we looked," Joe answered my question. I stood up from the couch. This was too much for me take in.

"I have to process this. I gotta go." I walked toward the door. My mother walked behind me.

"Please Lauren, please hear me out. I never stopped looking for you. I couldn't eat, sleep, or think straight for years. I lost so much weight worrying about you. I don't want you to go," she pleaded, but I couldn't stay there another minute.

"Please take my number." She scrambled for a pen and paper. I stood there feeling weaker by the second. I ran out of the house after I took the sheet of paper with her name and number on it.

I wasn't sure where I was going, but I knew I had to get there and fast. Everything I knew about my dad was a lie. He wasn't this great guy, shielding me from a woman who broke his heart. He made me grow up hating my own mother, thinking she was heartless and didn't want me. He made me believe she broke his heart and even worse that he rescued me. I sat in my car, crying tears of devastation.

Time to Face Reality
Tori

When Lauren came over I had been sitting in the house with all the curtains drawn and all the lights out. I called out of work for the next three days. I could live without my stuff, house, car and job, me and Misha did it before when I first graduated and was looking for a job. She went to work and held down the bills in a small one bedroom apartment. What I couldn't live without is the one woman who understood all of me. I talk a lot of shit about her attitude but it's what attracted me to her in the first place. Misha was exciting, she knew how to love me and though I now understood why she was distant she wasn't always that way.

After I slammed the door in Lauren's face I watched her drive away before I walked back over to the couch. My cell phone rang again and I was set on ignoring it until I saw my favorite picture of Misha appear on the screen.

"Hello," I answered with a small bit of hope.

"Tori, I left a few things at the house that I need to get. I'm informing you so you won't say I broke in."

"Ok, when are you coming?" I was anxious to see her.

"Within an hour," she said before disconnecting the call. I knew she thought I was at work. I hadn't taken a shower yet so I jumped up and ran to the bathroom. It only lasted five minutes before I jumped out and threw on a clean pair of boxers, basketball shorts, and a t-shirt. I threw the dishes in the sink and wiped down the kitchen table.

I tried to come up with several angles I could use to get her to stay and talk to me. None of them actually made sense especially knowing how my wife was. An hour and a half later I could hear someone lifting the small plant on the outside of the door and putting a key through the keyhole.

She froze for a minute when she saw me sitting on the couch.

"I can come back. I thought you were at work." She went to close the door, but I jumped up.

"No, it's ok, you can get what you need," I answered.

"Was I interrupting something?" She looked around like she half expected to see Lauren standing in the shadows.

"No, I called off work?" I confessed. Misha's face contorted into a frown.

"You never call out," she said as she closed the door.

"I know." I wanted to hug the shit out of her.

"Well, I'll only be a minute." She started walking toward the fireplace and grabbed the pictures of her wearing her wedding dress on our wedding day. She put the picture of us both back on the mantle.

"What are you doing?" I asked out of curiosity.

"I didn't step out on the marriage, so I figured I wanted the pictures of me on our wedding day." She didn't sound upset just resigned to the end of us.

"Misha, please sit with me for a second. Come on I know I fucked up, but I need you, I need us." I was willing to resort to begging if it meant she stays.

She stopped for a minute and said, "I honestly can't look at you the way I used to. Believe me I want to, I want to act like I don't remember shit, but I can't so let's just move on ok?"

I stood up and without thinking I wrapped my arms around her. She tried to push me off, but I didn't care I kept hugging her. Then I kissed her on her neck and her cheek stopping seconds away from her lips.

"Tori, stop ok? You can't possibly think I want to have sex with you. You must be crazy." She kept talking, but her body wasn't pushing me away the way her words were. I didn't answer only pressed my lips against hers softly. She twisted initially but melted into my kiss moments later. I used the tip of my tongue to trace her lips.

If she wasn't willing to hear my words, I would tell her how much I needed her to stay with the stroke of my dick. I parted her lips with my tongue with little resistance she complied. My hands roamed down to her back side as I used my strength to lift her up off the floor. Misha's legs wrapped around my waist and that was the only confirmation I needed. I wouldn't rush, but I needed to use my time wisely. She kissed me hungrily and started to kiss my neck and shoulders. I missed the hell out of her and wanted to show her. I laid her gently on the couch and slid her dress above her ass. With my right hand I eased her panties down until her wetness was exposed.

She moaned as my tongue met her clit and I used it to brush I love you into her sweet spot. I sucked her into my mouth softly, feeling her body tense up from pleasure. I was in my zone and nothing was going to stop me from making things right. Moments into sucking and licking my wife's wetness a knock on the door made me freeze. I was going to ignore it until the person knocked one more time. I prayed to God it wasn't Lauren again.

"You should get that. I probably should get going." Misha sat up on her elbows. I wasn't letting her go anywhere.

"No, hold on a minute." I stood up and wiped my mouth with my hand before heading over to the front door. I looked out the window, but only saw the back of a man's shoulder. He was wearing a black suit. I figured it was a Jehovah's Witness and planned on telling them to leave right away.

When I swung the door open, a familiar face looked at me with great disdain. It was Arnold Blake standing on the other side of the door with a manila envelope in his hand.

"Tori Carter?" he asked like he didn't know.

"What?" I asked rudely.

"I'm here to serve you divorce papers my man. You should know not to fuck with me." He shoved the envelope into my hands and walked away. I looked over my shoulder at Misha, surprise written across my face. I already knew she was serious about the divorce, but having that arrogant bastard deliver me the papers made me furious. I tried to calm myself as I slammed the door and remembered that right now the ball was in her court.

"What's this?" I asked.

"Tori, I didn't expect to come here and get wrapped up in sex. I just wanted to get my things and leave," she explained herself as she stood up from the couch.

"Why him Mish? Why did you want to use him to pay me back?" I asked with sincere hurt.

"I should go. We'll be scheduling a meeting with you and your lawyer for next week." She walked toward the door. I reached for her arm.

"Misha? I don't want a divorce," I told her with a straight face.

"I didn't want one either," her words weren't meant to slap me, but it didn't stop them from hurting anyway.

"Can we do counseling?" I threw it out there knowing that I was grasping at straws, but I was willing to try it all. She paused for a moment like she was considering it.

"I'll think about it. Bye Tori." She stepped out the door and I followed her. I watched as she walked over to a new looking Altima. I didn't want to know how or where she got it. It was time to visit my mother she would know exactly what to say to make me feel better.

Thrown Through a Loop
Misha

Things didn't go according to my plan. I was not supposed to be laying on the couch getting licked up by the man I was serving divorce papers. I wasn't sure what to feel, but Tori was taking me through a loop. I was starting to feel confused about getting a divorce especially with him throwing around words like counseling. I wasn't sure I was able to forgive him for cheating with Lauren, but I wasn't too sure about walking away from my marriage either. Being so attracted to him didn't help. Tori was the business, in and out of the bedroom and a divorce felt so final.

I sat in my rental contemplating my next step. I showed Tori weakness, but I knew it couldn't happen again. I thought about how many times he left the house randomly and wondered if he was actually going to see her. I could probably deal if it wasn't with Lauren, but her smug ass already has it all so having my husband shouldn't have been an option. I was reluctant to drive off and I guess Tori could sense it because he walked over to the driver's side and tapped the glass.

I rolled the window down slowly.

"Yes?" I asked more confused than I was previously.

"I know you don't want to go and you don't have to." He looked sexy standing over the car, his sexy dark brown eyes begging me to stay.

"I had a moment of weakness Tori, but I can only see Lauren on top of you and I doubt that image fades any time soon. I'm sure you loved me before, but now," My words were interrupted by the screeching of tires and a black Jaguar parking suddenly behind me. Lauren jumped out of the car looking devastated before reaching out for Tori. She stopped abruptly after noticing me sitting in the car. Our eyes locked, both giving the other the stare of death. Tori pushed Lauren away from him first, breaking us from our trance.

"Lauren, why the fuck are you here? Seriously, I told you already I'm done!" he shouted at her. She looked like she couldn't really hear him.

"I need to talk to you. It's important I swear, why is she here?" she asked like she really must have bumped her damned head.

"Cause she's my wife," Tori answered incredulously.

"I'm leaving," I yelled out the window before rolling it up. I couldn't believe this bitch was still trying to come around like she was claiming him.

"No, wait!" Tori yelled. He reached for the car door, but it was locked.

"I really need you Tori, please." Lauren looked desperate, so I'm sure if she was willing to get her ass beat it must have been for a good reason. I pulled away leaving

Tori looking after me in disbelief. I also didn't want to get in any more legal trouble until I was cleared.

Seeing her grimy ass there made me want to kill her all over again though. I didn't look in my rearview mirror until after I turned the corner. My mind was racing and I needed something to help me cope with the mess that was now my life. I called my friend Vivian to see if she wanted to go shopping. If I didn't distract myself now, I was sure to turn around and run Lauren's ass over. She said yes and I told her I'd be there in less than an hour. A text came through, but I didn't look at it

Nowhere Else to Turn
Lauren

I was too damn distraught to care about Misha sitting in front of Tori's house. I didn't have her anymore to share this bombshell with so Tori was the only person I knew who could help me. After Misha's car pulled off, Tori turned toward me angrily.

"You can't be serious?" He tried to walk by me but I grabbed his wrist.

"Tori, please, I really need you." I spoke through tears. He yanked his hand away and continued to walk toward his front door while texting a message on his phone.

"I was there for you through all of your shit and I need you now," I shouted in the street causing him to stop in his tracks.

He turned around slowly and grudgingly said, "Alright come in."

I followed behind him into his house and sat on the couch. I relayed all of what happened with my mother. His face softened as I cried out the details. He sat beside me on the couch and wrapped his arms around me.

"Damn, that's a lot right there." He spoke into my hair. He smelled good, completely different from earlier this afternoon. I felt the sting of jealousy that he cleaned himself up for Misha, but not me.

"I know, I'm not sure what I should do. I can't look my dad in the face anymore." I wiped away tears with my fingertips.

"You should tell him how you feel and that it wasn't cool for him to do what he did and then keep you from your mom all this time." Tori gave it to me straight, but I knew I wouldn't be able to say that to my father without wanting to scratch his eyes out.

"I mean I didn't even know he had a brother. He told me he was an only child and my grandparents passed away. Who the hell is he? Is all I keep asking myself." I was still upset, but was happy for Tori's company.

It felt so good resting my head on Tori's chest. I wanted to stay there forever, but he eventually pulled away.

"I know you need me right now, but I really have my own shit to worry about," he spoke, but I kissed him before he could finish his sentence. He didn't reciprocate, but he didn't move either.

"Listen Lauren, Arnold came to my house today." Tori looked me in my face for a reaction. I was shocked as hell and couldn't imagine why the hell he would do that.

"What? For what?" I asked confused.

"To serve me divorce papers. Misha went to him to be her divorce attorney." My heart jumped in my throat. Arnold hasn't called me all day and if Misha went to him he knew I was fucking around with Tori.

"Shit, shit, shit. What did he say?" I asked with panic written across my face. Arnold was a major investor in my club and he just had two big time investors give me money to help me expand.

"He told me that I should have never fucked with him which means he's going to come for my throat." Tori looked agitated. This was all happening so fast. When it rained it poured was the perfect saying.

I need to think about my next move or things could go from bad to worse in a matter of minutes. Tori stood up first and I followed. All of this was foreign to me, I never cared about anybody, but my damn self.

"I'm going to fix this." I made a promise I wasn't too sure I would be able to up hold.

"I don't know if you can." Tori looked sad as he walked over to the door. I was a little hurt that he was kicking me out, but I decided to go without a fight. Things could get really bad quickly. Before I walked through the door, I stopped and gave him another kiss. My tongue lightly traced his lips before sucking gently on his bottom lip. I could feel the lady killer getting harder. I smiled knowing I could still get him hard. I wrapped my arms around his waist.

"Lauren, we can no longer get down like that." He pushed me away and closed the door behind me. I felt angry, lost, and broken all at the same time. It was getting dark outside and I felt too lonely to go back to my big house.

I sent Chris a quick text asking what he was doing. He answered nothing and I asked if he wanted to hang out. When he agreed I told him to meet me in front of the club in a half hour. I drove in the direction of Club Seduction ready to break down but refused to. Chris was parked out front when I got there. As soon as I parked I checked myself in the mirror. He walked over to the driver side and opened my door for me.

"Come on get out," he instructed me. I stepped out of the car.

"I'm driving you now." He walked me around to the passenger side and closed the door for me before walking around to the driver side. I never realized exactly how sexy Chris was. His tall dark chocolate frame was all muscle and his short curly black hair was just right for running your fingers through. He was a smooth brother with a perfect white smile. I looked out of the window to distract myself. I need to clear my head.

"Where are we going?" I asked softly. I really didn't care where he took me as long as I was with someone.

"You'll see." He looked my way briefly. He drove me to a rural neighborhood with beautiful houses. We were going away from the city, so I knew he wasn't taking me out to eat not that I would be able to if I tried. When the car finally pulled into a driveway we were in front of a large brick front, two car garage, a sprawling front lawn leading up to a gorgeous dark wood door.

"Where are we?" I asked confused.

"My house," he stated proudly.

"Wow Chris, it's beautiful." I complimented half-heartedly. I never really knew how well he was living. I paid him well, but he must have a side hustle going on. He jumped out to open my door. I stepped out and grabbed my purse. I followed him to his front door looking around as we entered.

His crib was beyond nice with a marble floor in the vestibule leading to a very open floor plan.

"We can go in here, but give me a hug." He leaned in to hold me and I didn't resist. He wrapped his arms around my waist and I rested my head on his chest. I pretended he loved me for a moment and ignored all the other shit happening in my life right now.

"What's going on?" He asked into my hair, not letting me go.

"Everything." I didn't mean to cry, but my voice cracked and I buried my face into his hard chest. He didn't say anything just let me wet his shirt with my tears. When I was done, he took me by the hand.

"Come on sit down," he said.

"I didn't know you was living the high life." I tried to lift the mood in the room.

"It's a lot of shit you don't know about me." He smiled in my direction.

"I can see that." I wiped the remaining remnants of tears from my eyes and slid out of my shoes before sitting Indian style on his oversized couch.

"Tell me more then," I stated.

"Well, I know that you're upset and I'm just the dude to make that fade," he smiled, "You thirsty?" he continued.

"Yes please, do you have a pint of tequila, Jack Daniels, or Vodka straight, no ice?" I answered sarcastically.

He laughed on his way into the kitchen.

"No, but I do have ginger ale." He threw over his shoulder.

"Ok." I took a moment to look around some more. There were a few pictures of Chris with a little boy and girl around five and six years old. I didn't know he had kids. When he came back in the room, I decided to ask about it.

"Are they your kids?" I asked. He looked in the direction of my finger.

"Naw, they're my niece and nephew. They come to visit a few weeks out of the summer." He sat beside me. I was impressed.

"Why haven't we hooked up?" I surprised even myself with the question. Chris looked like he was thinking it over.

"Well first, you pay me and second I didn't think I was your type," he answered frankly.

"I understand, you are my type, but your first point stopped me before." He passed me the glass of ginger ale, but I leaned forward and kissed him. With no hesitation Chris kissed me softly at first then insanely intense.

Without thinking I turned into Chris and kissed him some more. He took the glass and set it on an end table. I sat on his lap and rubbed my fingers through his hair while our lips explored each other. I wasn't sure what I was about to do, but I needed the rejected feeling to fade away fast. I want to feel like someone cares about me.

"You sure about this?" Chris asked between kisses. I nodded my head yes and pulled his shirt up. He helped me pull it over his head before relaxing into the couch. I closed my eyes and kissed him softly. His lips were incredibly soft, his chest incredible muscular, and his now rising lower region now incredibly hard. I loved knowing he was attracted to me. I felt powerful again even if for only a moment.

Chris put his hands up to my face and began to wipe tears away. I didn't realize I was crying again until then. He wrapped his arms around me and whispered into my head.

"Its ok baby girl, now ain't the right time." I relaxed into his arms and we set in silence.

Stranger Than Reality
Tori

When Lauren left, I thought I would be able to collect myself but all I could think of is how bad Lauren's timing was. I could tell Misha wanted to come back in. We could have probably made love and talked this shit out, but that possibility rolled away with the silver Altima Misha was riding around in. I walked up to my bedroom and dropped on the bed to think about my situation. If I didn't make a move to save my marriage, I was looking at a bitter divorce that would leave me unfocused, unmotivated, and drowning in depression, no doubt. I laid across the mattress, staring up at the ceiling trying to think of what it would take for me to win over my wife. It wasn't long before I was drifting off to sleep.

"Tori? Tori? It's me baby, you know you still want me." I looked over in the direction of the familiar voice to see Lauren sitting on her bed. She wore a see through red

lace teddy that revealed her round tits. Her legs were crossed and she used her index finger to call me over seductively. I tried to fight the temptation, but she looked sexy as hell. I walked over to her and got on one knee. Lauren spread her legs for me to position myself between her pretty brown thighs. I leaned in for a familiar, but new kiss. She tasted sweet like chocolate dipped in caramel. My lips explored hers as I parted them with my tongue. She gently sucked my tongue while exploring my body with her fingers. I missed this touch, I could feel her desire with each stroke of her fingertips.

I kissed down her chin and stopped at her neck. Moans of pleasure escaped her throat. I let my lips trace kisses down her collarbone and over her cleavage. Both hands now massaging the soft mounds of flesh with hardened nipples. My desire for Lauren grew in intensity. My dick now standing at full attention. I stood up, towering over her and began to remove my clothes. She helped strip away my belt and pants. My lady killer fully erect and ready to penetrate her softness. Lauren pushed me onto the bed on my back after sliding out of her red lace thongs. Soft thighs surrounds my waist as she straddles me. She slowly sat on my hardness causing my abs to tighten. Right when she caught her stride, moving in circles on my lap the door opened. I turned in the direction of the entrance to find Misha standing in the doorway wearing a black trench coat. Fear gripped my chest, but I was unable to move. She unraveled the belt to her jacket and let it fall open. Her nakedness filled my eyes and made my dick grow an inch longer. Her jacket fell to her feet before she walked seductively over to me. It appeared she didn't see Lauren or she really didn't care.

She crawled cat like onto the bed and began kissing me softly. Her fingers rubbed across my chest, Lauren continued moving in circles. I reached for Misha's hair as we kissed. It felt good to kiss my wife. I needed to feel her, without notice Misha straddled my face brushing her neatly shaven wetness onto my lips. I lapped at her wetness softly then hungrily like I was starving. I allowed my tongue to do the convincing as I sucked on her clit. Misha moaned as she rode my face, reaching down to massage my head.

Lauren began riding me harder, more intense. It caused me to reach down to hold her by the waist. I wanted to enjoy Misha, but the intensity of Lauren's bouncing was distracting me.

"Tori, fuck me. Fuck this pussy, baby." Lauren began talking the way I liked. Her words were bringing me closer to a climax. Misha looked down at me and grabbed my head firmly.

"Eat your wife, you're the best to ever do it. Please Tori give it to me." Misha spoke over Lauren's moans of pleasure.

"Tori, right there, give it to me." Lauren spoke louder. Misha slid off of my face and leaned down for

another kiss. She sucked my bottom lip. Lauren stood from my hardness and leaned over to kiss my neck. Both women now fighting for a chance to kiss my lips. Misha moved back and reached for my hand pulling me to a sitting position. She laid back on the bed and pulled me over top of her. I swung her legs on my shoulders and began plowing away at her warm, tight pussy. Lauren grabbed me by the chin and kissed me as I stroked my wife. She pulled away and smiled.

*"Tori, baby. I need you." Misha spoke from beneath me causing me to look her way. I smiled before Lauren yanked my face back in her direction. They both shouted, "**CHOOSE!**"*

I jolted awake with sweat forming around my brow. That was the most bizarre dream I have ever experienced. The one thing that was sure was it left me more confused than before. I wanted to save my marriage. I didn't want to lose my wife, but I couldn't shake the attraction I had toward Lauren. I had to face the reality that I fell for her for a reason. A few weeks ago I made peace with the loss of my marriage to Misha and was all set on giving me and Lauren a real shot at being together, but now I was in an emotional battle that could leave me more broken than healed.

I jumped up from my bed to use the bathroom. I needed to see Misha before this divorce proceeding went too far. I looked in the mirror not completely recognizing the man that stared back. Splashing water on my face to wake me up completely I towel dried with a hand towel. I sent Misha a quick text asking if she would be willing to meet me at the park around the corner from my mom's house. It's the same park I used to take her to when we were teenagers. I didn't know if she would respond, but I had to give it a shot.

Unlikely Circumstances
Misha

I was still reeling after leaving Tori's house as I drove over to pick up my girl -Vivian. I needed to do something to distract my ass and fast. I hated the idea of Lauren winning especially since she had everything else. Greedy bitches always want more. I stopped at a red light, grateful for a few brief seconds of not moving. A black suit caught my eye. It was Arnold sitting alone at an outdoor café. I beeped the horn twice to get his attention. When he looked up, I waved. He stood up and walked toward my car. I looked for a place to pull over, finding a park a few feet away I pulled to a stop.

"Hey, thanks for hand delivering it," I thanked him.

"No problem, it felt good. How're you holding up?" he asked like he was genuinely concerned.

"I'll be fine," I lied. I didn't tell him that I was having second thoughts. That Tori mentioned counseling and two seconds before he arrived my soon to be ex-husband was face deep in my va-jay-jay.

"I'm setting up a meeting with one of my junior associates. They are skilled in divorce proceedings. I'm also here if you'd like to talk." He slid me a business card with both his numbers on it.

"Thanks, I'll keep that in mind. I only wanted to say thank you, didn't want to keep you from your lunch date." I looked behind him toward the table he just left.

"You weren't interrupting me I'm actually eating alone. You're free to join me," he asked politely.

"No thanks, I'm off for some retail therapy with a friend. Thanks for the offer though." He reached for my hand and kissed it before walking back in the direction of his table. That was weird, but I guess he felt sorry for me.

Thirty minutes later, I was pulling in front of Vivian's apartment complex. She came jogging out like someone out of teen dream magazine. I wasn't sure how she managed to look like a woman barely over eighteen.

"You ok honey?' She gave me a hug after sitting in the passenger seat.

"Yeah, I'll be fine." I hated feeling like a charity case. Vivian knew I was getting a divorce, but I didn't give her any of the gruesome details. I didn't know who to trust anymore. As I drove in the direction of the nearest shopping mall I listened to her tell me about her teaching job. She was an elementary school teacher. I laughed at some of the stories. Bad ass kids always had a way of cheering me up.

After spending nearly five hundred dollars on clothes and new shoes, we sat down to eat at the food court. Over a Caesar salad I shared with her parts of the ridiculous events of the last few months.

"I knew Lauren was no good. I'm sorry Misha, but I saw how flirty she was at the Christmas party your mom had a few years ago. You poor thing, do you need anything?" Vivian reached across the table to hold my hand. I shook my head no trying to fight back tears. How stupid was I not to notice Lauren checking out my man way back then.

"Now I have to look for work and start my damn life all over again. But I have a great divorce lawyer and I'm taking him for everything he has," I continued with my rant.

"Good for you, how is Tori acting after all this?" She probed further.

"He wants me back. He's been apologizing and even mentioned counseling. A part of me feels confused, but I'm not a dumb bitch and I refuse to look like a fool, not for him or anybody else." My voice elevated from frustration.

"Well, you don't have to rush, no matter what anyone else have to say it's your marriage and you can take all the time you need. If you think counseling will help, then go for it. If you think he may do it again or if you don't trust him anymore and that won't change then move on. I will say this though I know Tori loves you and I'm not sure why he allowed himself to walk into temptation, but I won't think you're a fool for staying." Tears rolled down my cheeks at my friend's words. I couldn't understand why I didn't hang out with Vivian more often, she was smart, funny, and knew how to uplift your spirit even when you thought it couldn't be uplifted.

We spent another thirty minutes in the food court eating and talking until we headed back to my rental in the mall's parking garage. A text came through before I turned on the ignition. Apart of me wanted to hit delete, but I read it. It was Tori asking if we could meet at the park around the corner from his mom's house. He is grasping at straws, I replied, FINE, in all caps to let him know I wasn't all too happy about it. I didn't tell Vivian I was planning to meet

Tori just dropped her off in front of her complex. She gave me another hug and told me to call her if I need anything. I had a feeling I would need her sooner than she thought.

I headed in the direction of my old neighborhood. It is funny how small things look when you get older. I pulled up slowly to the entrance of the park and looked around before parking. I saw Tori standing by a park bench wearing a pair of jeans that fell perfectly around his sneakers, a white t-shirt and a baseball cap turned backwards. If I wasn't so pissed, I would have thought he was good enough to eat. I stepped out of the car and walked over to where he stood.

"Hey Mish." He looked awkward almost like he wanted to put his arms around me, but realized this wasn't a friendly reunion.

""Hey." I sat down on the bench to avoid standing in front of him.

"Thanks for coming." He thanked me, but I wasn't sure how thankful he would be by the end of this meeting. He sat beside me on the bench. We both sat in silence for what felt like forever before I spoke up.

"Why'd you call me out here?" I asked directly.

"I just needed to see you. I feel like shit." He rubbed his hands together, resting his elbows on his thighs.

"Good, cause you should," I stated nonchalantly.

"I was serious about counseling. I'm willing to do whatever it takes to show you that I want our marriage. I did a real sucka move and I honestly regret it." He started to rant. I wasn't sure how much of it I actually believed. He was probably sorrier he got caught.

"Did you love her?" I asked without looking at him. I needed to know how deep their relationship went. He paused, I couldn't take his silence so I jumped up from the bench.

"DID YOU FUCKING LOVE HER?" I yelled at him. He looked me directly in the eye.

"No, I didn't love her," he answered, but for me the damage was done. He hesitated, which meant he could see himself falling for her.

"This shit was a bad idea. I shouldn't have come over here. Look, if you wanted to hurt me congratulations we're even. You paid me back." I turned to walk back to the car, tears welling in my eyes.

"Misha, stop being like that." Tori came up behind me and wrapped his arms around me. I started to cry, not because I was hurt, but because I hated that I still loved him.

"I didn't love her, but I was hurting too. I wanted you to take care of me, to treat me like you loved me. I love you Misha Carter from the first day I saw you walking home from school. I messed up, but let me fix it," He spoke into my hair. Those words were exactly what I needed a few weeks ago when he was done with me and now that I am ready to walk away he decides to give them to me.

"I'm sorry Tori, but I can't do this. Let me go." I yanked free and got in my car. I didn't stop to clear my head only started the car and pulled away. This was all too much for me to handle. The faster I do this divorce the faster I could get my life back on track without Tori.

Where do I go From Here?
Lauren

Hanging out with Chris was exactly what I needed. We made dinner together, cracked jokes, and watched a movie as we ate. I didn't realize how fun he could be. After the movie we both washed and dried the dishes and cuddled on the couch. I almost felt normal, like all of my problems were waiting outside of his house and weren't allowed to come with me inside. I fell asleep on his couch and he didn't bother to wake me up. Eventually, Chris dozed off with me.

It wasn't until I heard him whispering on his cell phone above my head that I opened my eyes again.

"I'm sorry, something came up. I know, I know. I'll make it up to you." He whispered into the mouthpiece. I shifted to let him know I was awake.

"Ok, I gotta go ok? I'll call you back in a little bit." He hit the end button and tossed his phone on the other side of the couch.

"Hey I'm sorry. I didn't mean to ruin your night." I sat up.

"It's cool, I had a good time," he responded.

"Maybe I should go, I don't want to get you in any trouble." I searched around for my shoes.

"Lauren, you don't have to leave. Stay with me." Chris reached out to grab my hand.

"You sure?" I asked again, not really wanting to leave.

"Yeah I'm sure. Come on I'll get you something to change in to." He stood up and started walking toward the stairs. I followed him to the second level of his gorgeous house. He had a king size bed resting on an espresso colored platform in the center of the room. The softness of his cream colored carpet was equivalent to walking on clouds. I sat on the bed and watched him search around in his dresser for a shirt for me to wear. Moments later he handed me a large white t-shirt and a pair of black basketball shorts.

"Sorry, I don't have anything from Victoria's Secret." He joked.

"I wouldn't wear it if you did. I'm not in the habit of posing in another woman's lingerie." I retorted with a smile on my face. He chuckled before turning his back as I stripped down to my panties and bra and slid into his clothes. The scent of bounty fabric softener filled my senses.

"So where will I sleep?" I asked with my clothes in hand.

"You can sleep in here. I'll sleep either on the couch or in one of my guest rooms. You done getting dressed?" Chris asked still facing the opposite direction.

"Yeah I'm all done. Thanks again." I placed my clothes on top of his dresser and walked back over to his bed. If his carpet were clouds, his bed was heaven. He walked toward the door and reached for the light switch.

"Goodnight." he started to walk away.

"Don't go. Sleep with me." I stopped him. I really didn't want to sleep alone tonight.

"You sure?" he asked with caution. I nodded my head yes and watched him walk in and close the door behind him. He removed his shirt revealing incredible arms and insanely sculpted shoulders.

"I'll behave, I just can't sleep with my shirt on," he explained but I was ok with it. When he slipped under the covers, I scooted toward him slowly and rested my head on his strong chest. He wrapped his arm around my waist until we both fell asleep.

The morning came in a blink of an eye and soon the sun came peeking through the windows. I stretched and turned to see Chris still sound asleep beside me. I looked down at him for an extra moment, wondering why I didn't try to get with him sooner. He really was good for me. Before he had a chance to wake up, I leaned down and kissed him on his lips very gently. I even closed my eyes for a brief second. He didn't move and I didn't want to disturb him, so I slipped out of bed quietly and grabbed my clothes from the dresser. I headed toward what I hoped was the bathroom to get dressed. The bathroom was huge with the shower separate from the bathtub. I slipped back into my clothes and folded his t-shirt and shorts leaving them on a small table by the bathroom door. I tip toed down the stairs and grabbed both my shoes and my purse.

  Chris was good to me, but I didn't want to lead him into my drama especially since I was still wrapped up in Tori. I opened the front door and sat on the one step to call a cab. I took a quick glance at my cell to check the time. It was only seven o'clock, but there were a few unanswered text messages blinking on my phone screen. Before I read anything, I sent Chris a thank you for last night text and. The cab came within twenty minutes. I waited patiently for it to arrive, thinking about everything I would need to do to repair my life. Once the cab arrived, I sat in the back and gave him the address to Club Seduction so I could get my rental car.

With no morning traffic we were there in no time. I gave him two twenties and told him to keep the change. The BMW looked untouched so I retrieved my keys and got inside. The ride home was a quiet one. After pulling into my parking spot I took several deep breaths. Being at Chris' was like going on vacation and now I must face my reality.

I retrieved my texts before heading into the house and one was from an unknown number. It read: I missed the first time, but I damn sure won't the second. The message sent chills up my spine. I was scared to read the second message, but it was from my dad asking if I wanted to meet for lunch. I wasn't sure when my life started unraveling, but it was quickly turning into a pile of yarn. I couldn't look my dad in the face right now so I sent a quick text asking for a rain check. I needed to meet with Arnold to repair the damage done by Misha.

I looked over my shoulder before unlocking my door. A quick scan of the room didn't show any signs of being tampered with. I was becoming paranoid. I walked slowly into my downstairs bedroom and looked to see if anything was out of place. It wasn't, so I set on my bed to think. I didn't want to call Arnold because then he might not answer, but if I showed up to his office I risked him not being there. I shot him a text asking if we could meet at our favorite hotel around noon. It took a few minutes, but he responded with a yes.

I walked to my shower and stripped down to nothing. Warm water sprayed from the powerful jets in the shower head. I stepped in to a small piece of serenity. My shower lasted for a good thirty minutes before I stepped out into the open bathroom. Standing in my closet used to be fun, but now I only saw a large box with colorful material. Nothing was making sense. I selected a hip hugging black dress with a dangerously low neckline, matched it with a pair of red heels to match my new red lipstick. I placed my outfit out on the bed. Despite my gloomy life, I found myself horny as hell. I decided that would work to my advantage with Arnold. I was sure he was going to be pissed, but as of right now he doesn't know that I know.

With nothing on but a robe I ate a bowl of cereal on the couch when my cell rang. It was Chris.

"Hey Chris." I answered with a smile plastered on my face.

"When did you leave?" he asked still a bit groggy.

"Around seven. I didn't want to wake you." I took another bite of Raisin Bran.

"I was planning on making you breakfast." He spoke in a low sexy tone.

"Maybe next time. I think you're trying to seduce me," I flirted.

"Is it working?" he asked playfully.

"Have a good day Chris. You're so silly, but it is working." I confirmed his suspicion, not wanting it to stop. I watched a few reality shows until it was almost time for me to leave. It's so funny how the right outfit can make you feel like a million bucks. I instantly felt great seeing myself in the mirror, almost like I forgot my visit was potentially hazardous. My only line of defense would be my sex appeal. I would try to seduce him into forgiveness, after all he was also a married man.

I parked in my usual spot at our favorite hotel and went into the reception area to reserve the same room I've had since I've started seeing Arnold. Without any question Carolyn the receptionist booked my room, handed me my keycard, and told me to enjoy my stay. I walked over to the elevators like I had no care in the world. It was fifteen minutes before noon and Arnold was usually early so I expect him to get here soon.

Like clockwork two knocks sounded on the other side of the door.

"Who is it?" I asked like usual.

"Your man," Arnold spoke like he wasn't upset, which could mean one of two things. That he was extremely mad or that he was going to get even. I decided to play it cool and quickly stepped out of my clothes before opening the door completely nude aside from my heels. He was taken off guard and stood in the doorway for a minute to examine my assets.

"What are you doing?" he asked while stepping inside.

"Nothing, do you like?" I flirted with him.

"Of course." He closed the door behind himself and wrapped his arms around my waist for a kiss. I kissed him with intense passion. Like I haven't seen him in days. Arnold's interest in me lies in the details. His wife doesn't take the time to appreciate what he does. He likes me to flirt with him, to treat him like I need him, and act like I understand his contribution to my success. He never told me what he wants just what he doesn't get at home, so I embodied what he's missing.

"I've missed you." I continued to dote on him, planting strategic kisses against his cheek and neck.

"You have, have you?" he asked with a hint of sarcasm.

"Yes, let me show you how much." I stepped back. I could see the bulge in his pants growing.

"Before you show me, why don't you explain to me why I'm hearing about you fucking Tori?" He grabbed me by the arms and shook me with each word. I was shocked to say the least, he's never handled me that way before.

"Arnold you're hurting me. Let me go." I looked him in the eyes.

"What is it, huh? I haven't given you enough? I'm not pleasing you?" He pushed me back on the bed forcefully. Tears welled in my eyes.

"Arnold, it's not that," I started.

"Then what is it? He gets to come to your house, so I know he means more than me," he started yelling with anger.

"It was a mistake and I know that. I don't want him baby. You are the only man for me." I lied. I didn't want the situation to escalate, so I needed to calm him down. I stood up from the bed and walked in front of him. "Arnold, I promise, I will never do that again." I kissed him on his lips softly. He turned his head, but I continued to kiss him all over his face.

"Stop Lauren, you don't mean that shit." His tone was softer, not as angry so I kept kissing him.

"I do mean it. You are all the man I need. You were so busy honey and I felt lonely. I never meant to hurt you." I planted kisses on his neck until he finally wrapped his arms around me. I thought his anger subsided when he began removing his clothes. Once naked however, he grabbed me by the waist and yanked me around. He pressed his hardness into me forcefully, one hand reached around to my neck and held me with a firm grip as he pumped harder and harder into me. I couldn't believe how intense he was. I just bit my bottom lip as a single tear rolled down my face. With stronger strokes, he began to talk.

"You-will-never-screw-me-over-again. Do-you-hear-me?" he asked seconds before his climax. He removed his hand from my neck and placed it on my waist as his body tensed, preparing for his release. Words were stuck in my throat at having been used like a cheap two dollar whore. He pushed me aside and dropped on the bed beside me.

Put Your Money Where Your Mouth is
Tori

After Misha left the park I drove around to my mom's house. I confessed my sins and I how I screwed things up. I told her what Misha told me about the adoption situation and how I was sleeping with Lauren before I even knew that. My mom told me she was disappointed with me for stepping out on my marriage and that just like I was done with the marriage Misha had every right to want to leave also. I told her that I didn't want to really divorce my wife, how I was willing to do what it took to save my marriage. She ended our conversation by saying this simple truth. "Then it's time for you to put your money where your mouth is." I knew she meant it was time for me to back up my words with action.

I started the car thinking about how I could prove to Misha that I wasn't done with my marriage. I had a few ideas and decided that I would start on them first thing in the morning. I only had two days off that I would dedicate to Misha full time. Instead of going home I rode a few blocks down from my mom's to Pete's lounge. It's a small hole in the wall bar that had a pool table. I found a parking spot close by and headed in the direction of the bar I grew up around but never spent too much time in.

The lights were dim and the room was filled with smoke. It was so thick you almost couldn't see anyone else there. I headed in the direction of the bar to get a beer before making my way back to the pool tables.

"Can I get a Corona?" I asked the short, brown skinned bartender. She looked me over with lust in her eye before handing me the bottle.

"That'll be five dollars." I handed her a ten and asked for another one. I threw three dollars into her tip jar and walked my beers to the back room.

"Hey Tori." An old friend greeted me on my way to the back.

"Hey man, how you been?" I asked, not really caring. The back room was filled with a few familiar faces and some not so familiar. The one thing that stood out to me was Misha's older brother Mark. He had his eye on me the entire time. I ignored him, but my gut told me I wouldn't be staying as long as I originally thought.
So much for clearing my head, I thought to myself. All the tables were occupied leaving me with no choice, but to take a seat to wait. Mark was playing a game against a mean looking dude.

I was sure Jerry's dumb ass already told Mark about what was going on with me and Misha, so I expected him to show out. I never had any problems with Mark, but the fact that he didn't speak let me know he knew. He polished the top of his stick as he walked around the table looking for the best angle. I took a swig of my Corona as the other men told jokes, talked shit, and made bets. If a table didn't free up soon, I promised myself I'd leave. I didn't feel like any shit from Mark and beating his ass wouldn't help me with Misha. Thirty minutes later and it didn't look like anyone would be giving up their table anytime soon. I drunk the last of my Corona and stood up to relieve myself before heading out.

"What you rushing for? It's not like you have a wife to run home to." Mark taunted in the background. I ignored him and kept going toward the men's room.

"Pussy, you heard me," Mark provoked. I turned to look at him.

"Go ahead with yourself man," I shot back at him. I didn't turn my back in case he had a bright idea.

"I heard what ya punk ass did to my sister." He walked toward me with the pool stick in his hand. I knew he was going to try to hit me with the stick, so I had my guard up and my eyes ready.

"What happened between me and my wife is my damn business." I looked him directly in his eye. A brief second later he raised the pool stick above his head and came down hard with it. I reacted quickly by stepping out of the way and reached for his shirt. I pulled him toward me and slammed his back against the wall.

"Look motherfucka, I didn't come here for no shit ok? I'm sorry about what happened with me and Misha, but I swear I will fuck you up if you ever swing at me again. Now take your drunk ass home." I pushed him hard into the wall and walked out with a group of onlookers looking confused. I didn't have time for this shit especially since I'm trying to fix my mistake.

I drove straight home and locked my car before stepping into my house. My adrenaline was still pumping from the encounter at the bar and I hated that I was coming home to an empty house. I watched a few college basketball games, made a sandwich before heading up stairs to go to bed. Nothing felt right anymore and I was irked that I lost everything within a matter of a few weeks. I was going to have to either fight for Misha or succumb to the realization that my marriage was over.

My alarm clock sounded at seven thirty, I hit the dismiss button angry that I forgot to turn off my alarm last night. I turned to see the empty space on the other side of the bed that used to have Misha there.

"Shit." I closed my eyes again but sleep had passed. *No point in sitting around,* I thought to myself. I got out of bed and shuffled to the bathroom. About this time Misha would be standing in the bathroom with me while I brushed my teeth asking if I wanted eggs or cereal for breakfast. She woke up with me every morning during the week to make me breakfast and to pack me a lunch. No matter what problems we had she always made sure I ate. I shook the thought from my mind and set out to accomplish my mission. I would have a dozen red roses delivered to her mom's house this morning. I was going to hand deliver a gift bag carrying a diamond bracelet she had her eye on with a greeting card housing five hundred dollars. I was trying to be creative because though Misha was a handful she wasn't very materialistic.

I ate breakfast waiting for a local floral shop to open, so I could place my order. While I ate I googled a few marriage counselors to see about making an appointment. I was leaving her with no opportunities to think about it or to say no. If she wanted a divorce, I would fight it every step of the way. I found an African American woman counselor who claimed to be in the marriage healing business and my marriage needed more than healing. I dialed the number and waited for an answer.

"Dr. Grace's office, how may I help you?" A cheerful female voice answered.

"Hello, I would like to make an appointment." I fought the desire to hang up. I didn't know anyone who spoke with a shrink.

"Great, may I have your name please?" the woman asked oblivious to my inner turmoil.

"Tori Carter."

"Will your spouse be attending or is this an individual session?" she asked.

"Uh, no this will be a couple's session." Though those words came out of my mouth I wasn't really sure if Misha would attend.

"Ok Mr. Carter, do you prefer weekday or weekend?" she continued her questioning.

"Tomorrow if I could." I knew I was pressing it, but drastic time's calls for desperate measures.

"Hold on a moment." The line went silent for a few minutes.

"I can fit you in at five tomorrow evening." She came back on the line.

"That will be fine. Thanks." We wrapped up our call with her giving me the address and taking down my credit card information. Sessions were $125 an hour, so I hoped she was good at what she does.

I hung up and ordered a dozen red roses and a single white rose to be placed in the center and went upstairs to take a shower. I needed to get to the jewelry store early if I planned on being at Misha's mom's before she could think about going anywhere. The shower felt so good I needed to talk myself out of it. I dressed in Misha's favorite t-shirt that showed off my muscular shoulders and arms, and a pair of ash gray jeans. I hopped in the car and headed over to Tiffany's I knew the bracelet was going to cost me, but losing my wife would be more expensive.

There was a parking space directly in front of the store. It didn't yet look open so I walked over to see the schedule listed on the door. I had another thirty minutes before they opened up. I sat in the car plotting on what to say when I got there. I remembered when Misha came to my mom's house looking to talk and how I let my sister take a swing at her. I felt bad for putting her threw it and wished I would have heard her out right then. None of this would have gotten this far and I would have called it quits with Lauren before we ever got caught. I was so lost in my thoughts I didn't see the petite blond haired woman opening the gate to the Tiffany's shop. Hearing the sound of the metal clamoring upward broke my train of thought. I would wait a few minutes to give the woman a chance to get herself together.

  A good fifteen minutes later and I stepped out of the car and walked toward the entrance. A chime indicated my entrance and the woman smiled politely in my direction.

  "How can I help you today?" she asked with a big smile across her face.

"Can I see your diamond bracelets please?" I asked while looking around.

"Sure, did you have something special in mind?" she asked on her way to the far right side of the store.

"Yes, I need something that says, I'm sorry," I confessed. With a knowing head nod she escorted me over to a glass case filled with sparkly diamonds.

"This is our best I'm sorry bracelet selection," she reassured. I took a look at a few of the bracelets until my eye caught a glimpse of a platinum bracelet trimmed in diamonds and a small diamond encrusted key dangling from the center.

"May I see that one?" I pointed out the bracelet and waited for her to take it out of the case. She sat it on the top of the glass counter for me to see.

"Wow, it's beautiful." I remarked. I turned over the tiny price tag to reveal a hefty $2,500. I didn't flinch for two reasons I thought Misha deserved it and second I didn't want the lady to see me sweat.

"I'll take it." I informed the woman of my decision and watched her face light up.

"Great, I'll go have it added to a gift box and be right back ok." She walked with the bracelet to a separate counter and placed it in a beautiful signature tiffany box with a white satin bow. I paid using my debit card and she handed me a small folder with my receipt and certification of authentication along with a teal gift bag with the bracelet inside.

"Have a good day and I'm sure she'll forgive you when she sees it." She tried to make me feel better.

"Thanks, I sure hope so." I took my items and walked back to the car. I needed to head over to the bank to withdraw the five hundred I wanted to give her. The bank was a few blocks up and empty when I arrived. I quickly withdrew the money and stopped at a gift shop where I bought a card with a sorry sentiment. I borrowed a pen from a cash register and wrote an apology with the date, time and address of the appointment tomorrow inside of the card. I hoped this worked.

With nothing left to buy or do I headed in the direction of my mother in law's house. My heart started pounding out of my chest the closer I got. My phone pinged indicating I had an email. At the red light I checked and it was the floral shop indicating my flowers were delivered. That made me feel a bit better. Hopefully they put her in a better mood. When I pulled up, her brother Jerry's car wasn't there which was a good sign. I took a deep breath, reached for the Tiffany gift bag from the glove compartment and grabbed the card and headed to the front door. I took a deep breath and rang the bell while convincing myself not to run off the porch.

My mother in law answered the door semi-surprised to see me.

"Is Misha home?" I asked with my gift hand behind my back. My mother in law looked sympathetic, but didn't gesture for me to come in.

"Hold on." She closed the door and I could hear her call for Misha. Moments later the door opened again and I saw my wife wearing her hair in a messy ponytail. She wore a pair of grey and pink yoga pants and a white t-shirt. I knew from her clothes she was just waking up not too long ago.

"Hi." I started.

"Hey." She stepped onto the porch and closed the door behind her.

"I won't take up much of your time."

"I hope you don't think flowers are going to change my mind." She went in for the kill.

"I know they won't I just wanted to let you know that I am really sorry and that I'm not giving up on us. Here." I extended my hand with the Tiffany bag. I could see a twinkle in her eye pass quickly. She took the bag, but didn't go to open it.

"Please open it." It's crazy, but I wanted to see her expression, I figured I could at least gage her level of anger.

"I will, later," she said slightly sarcastic. She knew I wanted to see her face but she wanted to torture me.

"Come on please, I'm trying Misha I really am."

"Okay, but it's not going to change anything Tori." She opened the bag and took out the box. Her eyes lit up when she saw the bracelet. She looked over the certification paper briefly. She pulled out the card and took it out of the envelope. Surprise registered when she spotted the money. I knew she wasn't expecting that, but I knew she may have a few things she needed to take care of. She stopped to read the card and tears welled in her eyes.

"I don't expect it to change anything, but I want you to see that I'm fighting for us. I was dead wrong and there is nothing I wouldn't do to take it back. Just think about it ok? I'll be there tomorrow I hope you are too." I was happy she didn't kick me off the porch in a rage. She just looked at me for a moment with tears in her eyes.

"I don't." I interrupted her not giving her a chance to turn me down.

"I'm going to leave, don't answer me now just think about it." I kissed her on the forehead and walked back toward my car. It wasn't until I got in my car that I noticed her sitting on the porch reading the card again. I felt like shit, but at least she knew where I stood. I left her to think about the appointment and hoped she came. If she didn't show up I knew we were over.

Decisions Decisions
Misha

I heard the doorbell ring, but didn't think it was for me. Moments later my mom called me into the kitchen to look at the large and beautiful bouquet of red roses with a single white rose in the center. I knew that Tori was telling me I was the only thing pure in his heart. We did the same arrangement on our wedding day. I had to admit it touched me in spite of how angry I was. When he left me sitting on the porch, I could only stare at the card showing an appointment for a counselor. He wasn't a go to therapy kind of guy, so I knew he was serious enough to actually make the appointment. When he pulled off, I walked in the house and tossed the gift bag on the kitchen table before flopping down in a chair.

"It's tough I know, but God will give you the strength you need to stay strong." My mom rubbed my back, which helped promote my tears.

"But Mama, God doesn't like divorce and I'm conflicted," I confessed through tears.

"Honey, people say that, but God says the only time divorce is ok is when someone steps out on their marriage. The choice is yours and I'm not going to tell you what you should do in either direction, but God won't be upset in this case. Misha you need to pray on this and ask God for guidance. Yes, Tori may be sorry, but it's not about him right now or even how he feels. What do *you* want to do? How do *you* want to proceed?" Mama preached to me and for the first time I didn't feel like I didn't want to hear it. Growing up my mother had so much advice, I didn't want to hear when I was a teen. Looking back on it, I realize that she was right about all of it.

When I got pregnant she wasn't upset, just told me that though she didn't condone my sin of fornication God blesses the womb. She said that I wasn't going to have an abortion to cover up the first sin, so I chose adoption to protect both Tori and I. I hated handing my child over to the nurses and it killed me to see them walk away with him. There was nothing that could eliminate the regret I had on that and seeing Tori with Lauren was the ultimate payback. However, I was beginning to think our 'sins' were equally wrong.

"You're right. I need to make up my mind even though it's hard. I just don't want to be one of these women who accepts a cheating husband and everyone thinks I'm a fool," I confessed. My mom sat in a chair facing me.

"Child please, most of us say what we wouldn't tolerate until it happens to us and then we find ourselves tolerating it. Don't live your life based on what you think others will say. Tori is a good man otherwise. However, I will say this, if you do take him back take your time let him see what he's lost. He has to feel his loss for him to never make the same mistake." She was right as always.

"Let me tell you something about your father." She continued. I sat at attention. It was a rare occasion for my mother to mention my dad so I listened up.

"When we were younger, right before you were born he started acting real different. He stayed out late, mood changes, and wanted to sleep a lot. When I confronted him with it, he tried to start a fight. I let him know clearly that my intuition told me he was stepping out. He looked at me real serious like and then confessed it. I didn't say anything just walked into our bedroom and took out his suitcase. When he asked where I was going, I told him nowhere but he was. I packed up all of his clothes and told him to leave. We didn't get back together for a year with him begging and pleading to come back home the entire time. I was pregnant with you a year later. He never cheated after that and apologized again right before he passed away. People will treat us how we let them. You were wrong about not telling him about the baby and he had a very good reason to be upset, but he cheated and now you are justified in your anger. Do what's best for you honey."

Right then I saw the humanness of my mother. I always saw her as a bible toting, God fearing angel, but today that story let me know she was a woman who loved a man and went through experiences and learned valuable lessons. I stood and kissed her on the cheek before going back upstairs into my room. I needed to hear that. After closing the door I looked at the bracelet again and tried it on before laying back on the bed. This was the bracelet I pointed out a few months ago and said I wanted it for Christmas. He got it for me which let me know he was paying attention.

The image of Lauren came flooding into my mind, moaning with pleasure from something that was supposed to be mine and I unfastened the bracelet and tossed it in the gift bag. *Damn you Tori,* I cursed him to myself. I decided that going to that therapy session would be a total waste of time. I refused to be a paranoid chick asking him where he was and what he was doing and with who. I couldn't live like that and I didn't want to become that girl especially with my attitude we would both be miserable. The money was right on time though, I needed to pay my credit card bill soon.

An hour later I could hear a few male voices talking down stairs so I went to investigate. It was my brother Mark and his best friend Eric talking to my mom.

"Hey Mark." I kissed him on the cheek.

"Hey Mish. What's up? How you feeling?" he asked.

"Nothing much. I've seen better days," I confessed. His friend Eric was looking me up and down. He's had a crush on me since grade school.

"Hey Eric," I greeted him nonchalantly. Though he was looking pretty good.

"Hey Mish. You looking good," Eric flirted which made Mark snap his neck in his friend's direction.

"Be careful man," Mark warned.

"Anyway Mish, Tori was in Pete's Lounge last night trying to catch a game of pool. I was about to lay it on him with my pool stick." Mark informed me. That was odd he never goes in there or so I thought it, it must have been when we finished talking.

"Yeah, you don't have to do that Mark," I informed my overprotective big brother. Mark was a bit of a lush so it was no surprise he was in the bar.

"Well I do, if you want me to," Eric continued to flirt.

"No thank you, but thanks for the offer. Mama let me know if you need help with lunch." I walked out of the kitchen and back upstairs. Mark and his friends were always getting into something and I was just glad Jerry was at work so they couldn't conspire to jump Tori. Though he let his ratchet ass sister ambush me, I wouldn't pay him back that way.

My cell started to ring with an unfamiliar number.

"Hello?" I asked

"Hello, may I speak with Misha Carter?" A male voice asked.

"This is she? May I ask whose calling?" I asked hesitantly.

"It's Barrett Miller, Mr. Arnold Blake assigned me to your divorce case. I wanted to speak with you about setting up a meeting," Barrett introduced himself.

"Oh right? Well, I'm free whenever."

"Ok, well I have an opening next Thursday afternoon if you're free then. Let me know I will send out a letter to Mr. Carter," Barrett continued. My heart stopped with the mention of me and Tori being in the same room with lawyers discussing the end of my marriage.

"Mrs. Carter? Will that be ok?" his question snapped me back into reality.

"Sure, yeah that will be fine."

I jotted down the time and suite number we were to meet in before ending the call. This was all starting to look so final. If I was going to go through with it I would need to start looking for a job and fast. I couldn't live with my mother forever despite how good her cooking was. I googled job openings in the area on my phone and started writing down info. I didn't have much to add to my resume, but I was a genius with creating all of my skills and how I applied them. My phone rang again and this time Arnold's number popped up on the screen.

"Hello."

"Hey Misha, just wanted to see if my associate Barrett gave you a call already?" he asked.

"He just did not too long ago actually. I made the appointment for next Thursday. Will you be there?" I asked.

"Yes, I will be there. Was I interrupting you?" Arnold asked with a hint of curiosity.

"No actually, I was just looking for a job." I was embarrassed to admit that.

"Oh really, you need work? One of my partners is looking for an assistant. Come down today and hand in your resume," he offered.

"You're so nice, but I actually don't have a resume. I spent most of my time taking care of my husband." I confessed feeling more and more foolish as the conversation wore on.

"Can you work a fax machine?"

"Yes."

"Can you send an email, type a letter, and put things in chronological order?" he asked.

"Yes."

"Then come down today and I will put in a recommendation for you. Be dressed to kill. He can't resist a beautiful woman," Arnold laughed and I followed.

"Well ok then, I'll see you in what in an hour and a half?" I asked.

"Sure, I'll be here." We both hung up with me thinking how wrong I was about Arnold the first time we all met in the restaurant. He was proving to be a real gentlemen. I jumped up from my bed and walked to my now small closet.

My eyes went to the black pencil skirt I just bought and a maroon colored lace camisole tank top. I matched it with a grey princess cut waist length blazer and my black strappy stilettos. I knew how to put it on when I had to. I took a quick shower, lotioned up, and sprayed on a dash of J-Lo's perfume before getting dressed. I couldn't believe I was going to get a job when I haven't worked in the last five or six years. I held down the house while Tori finished up college and looked for a job. We didn't have much student loan debt to repay because I researched the hell out of grants and fellowships he qualified for. When he finally got his current job making a little over eighty thousand a year with great benefits for us both, he said I didn't have to work for a while. He wanted to take care of me and the kids we were supposed to have. So despite my issues of guilt I cooked and cleaned my house to perfection. I sexed him up and after the two miscarriages and then I became depressed with my sins haunting my bedroom.

Tori never worried about a hot meal unless we had a super huge argument and then I told him to get the hell out of my face until he apologized. Knots grew in my stomach thinking that Arnold's partner might turn me down for a more experienced assistant. I wasn't going to let that stop me though, I would sashay into that office like I owned the damn place. I pulled my hair up into a bun and did my makeup as close to flawless as I could get. When I came back down stairs, my brother and his friend were both gone.

"Mama, I have an interview. I'll be back a little later." She turned to see me go.

"Well look at you! You look like a million and two dollars." We both shared a laugh as I headed out to the Altima. I checked my hair, teeth and makeup once more before pulling off toward Arnold's office. I wasn't sure how this would go, but I needed it to happen for me and fast.

I parked in a nearby parking spot a few doors down from his office and headed to Arnold's secretary. The same pleasant woman who greeted me the first time I was here said hello. I asked to speak with Arnold and she told me to wait by the waiting area. Moments later he came out wearing a tailor made gray suit, royal blue dress shirt, and black, silver and purple striped tie.

"Follow me please." He led me to his office with his right hand. I followed feeling a little less confident from our first encounter in this very office.

"I had a chance to talk with Peter Rosen on your behalf. I told him how efficient you are around the office and that you aren't bad on the eyes either." Arnold flashed me a million dollar smile. I was beginning to understand why Lauren chose him.

"Thank you so much for doing this," I thanked him.

"It's nothing, Pete was already telling me how badly he needs someone, so it'll be a good fit. He's already expecting you. Laugh at his jokes and smile a few times and you're good to go." Arnold stood up and escorted me to the office of Peter Rosen.

I knocked twice and was told to come in by a male voice. I entered a bit cautious. Peter was much more than I expected. A very handsome white male with black hair, green eyes, and a perfect white smile greeted me.

"I'm Misha, here about the job." I stepped into his oversized office.

"Yes, come in. Arnold told me you'd be here. Did you find me ok?" he asked with a warmth in his eye.

"Actually I did." His demeanor made me relax, he wasn't an uptight asshole I expected him to be. He asked me a few general questions about my ability to operate office equipment and answer phones. He flirted, smiled, and told a few jokes. I did as Arnold instructed and laughed politely at each of them. By the end of our meeting he was shaking my hand, telling me I start on Monday and how much I'd be making an hour. I couldn't believe how simple it all was. I wanted to kiss Peter on his cheek, but restrained myself. I left his office and made my way back over to Arnold's office.

"Hey, how'd it go?" he asked knowingly.

"It went perfect. I start on Monday. I can't thank you enough. I really needed this." I walked over to his desk and kissed him on the cheek.

"You're welcome. You're going through a tough time and I understand." He looked a bit surprised by my kiss, but didn't make a big deal.

He told me I could fill out all of the paperwork on Monday and he would have his assistant give me a quick training on the phone system. I was super excited that I would be able to get out of my mom's house sooner rather than later. I thanked him again and walked back to the car. I would need to celebrate, under normal circumstances I would suggest going out with Tori or calling up Lauren, but since they were both two timing back stabbers all I could think to do was tear up in the car. I was tired of feeling down about the two damn people I trusted most hurting me deeper than any knife wound.

Get your shit together Misha, I thought to myself before looking in the rearview mirror. I had money in my damn pockets, a car to cruise around in and a job to boot. I slapped a smile on my face and headed back to my house to change. I planned on getting turned up tonight and acting a fool. I sent Vivian a text treating her to a celebratory dinner. When she responded yes, I took off in the direction of my mom's house with nothing but the wind getting in my way.

The Devil's Playground
Lauren

Arnold made me feel like a two dollar hooker when he fucked me disrespectfully and he would soon pay, but for now I needed to save my club. I took a drive over to my club to oversee the work being done. My father was right about it not being as bad as I thought it would be and Chris did an excellent job of taking care of things. Contractors were busy at work on the front of the building. I parked in my usual spot and opened the back door where Chris was already waiting for me in my office. It felt a bit unsettling being there again after the fire.

"Hey pretty lady." Chris gave me a hug when I walked in.

"Hey handsome." I sat my purse down and slipped out of my shoes.

"Did the contractors give you a time frame they'd be done?" I asked over my shoulder.

"They said about two weeks. The firemen got here in enough time that no major damage was done. It's all cosmetic. I had the electrician here earlier and he gave me a green light as far as the electrical. We'll be up again and better than before." He smiled at me. I couldn't believe I would need to do another commercial saying I was back in business.

Chris and I discussed more business when a hard knock on the back door interrupted us. My heart froze, but Chris stood up and walked toward the door.

"Who is it?" he asked aggressively.

"It's Shannon." My dad's girlfriend spoke through the heavy metal door. I couldn't believe she was here.

"Let her in," I whispered. Chris unlatched the door and let Shannon in.

"I didn't mean to disturb you," she stated. People are funny is all I could think.

"Can I have a minute?" I asked Chris. He nodded his head and stepped out of the office closing the door behind him.

"What do you need?" I asked trying to cut through all of the bull shit.

"You haven't been answering your father's phone calls or texts, so I thought I'd check in on you." She stood in front of my desk now.

"Well, you can tell him I'm fine and that I will come over a little later this afternoon," I spoke nonchalantly.

"You don't think you're being a bit reckless Lauren?" she asked like she thought she had a right to.

"Let's get something straight ok? You're not my mother and never will be, so don't come to my place of business telling me I'm being reckless." The nerve of this bitch coming here to put me in check.

"You need to make sure you stay away from Arnold," she added with a threatening tone. Now it made sense she wasn't checking in on me for my dad, but protecting her sister's interest.

"Shannon, instead of being in my business you should go keep an eye on your own damn man. Now get out before I have you escorted the hell out." I gave it to her plain and simple and her face turned red like she might try something. I was ready for her though. With the week I've had I was liable to beat the shit out of her first and ask questions later.

She walked to the back door slowly before turning to warn me one last time.

"I'm just letting you know that you're messing with the wrong one, ok? Stay away from Arnold if you know what's best for you." With that she walked out of the office and the heavy metal door slammed behind her. I was done with all of this and I was going to confront my father when

I left the club about all of the nonsense I had piling up around me. Chris stuck his head in the office to be sure I was ok. I gave him a few more instructions and told him to call me if he needed anything. I looked at him differently now that we've spent the night together, but I needed to clear my head before going there.

On my way to my dad's I tried to coach myself into what I would say, but really wasn't sure how I would react to seeing him. It felt weird knowing that I grew up with a kidnapping ass rapist who was just daddy who loves me a week ago. Shannon's car wasn't there when I pulled into my father's driveway an hour later. I sat in my rental car for what felt like forever before building up enough courage to go to my dad's door. With a deep breath and a bit of anger I stormed up to his front door and rang the doorbell. Within a few moments he opened the door with a smile on his face.

"Hey baby girl, why didn't you use your key?" he asked nonchalantly.

"Because you're a stranger." I heard myself say it, but I couldn't really believe that I did. My heart pounded behind my chest filling my ears with its loud thumping sound.

"A stranger? What are you talking about?" He turned his back to walk in and I followed angrily behind.

"Well let's see, I thought you were an only child. I thought my mother cheated on you, shall I continue?" I forced myself to keep it going. My father's body turned around fiercer than I have ever seen him before.

"What did you say to me?" he asked with fire behind his eyes. It scared me, but I couldn't show it.

"I spoke to my mom and she told me what you did to her. She told me what you did to your brother." My hands were shaking. My dad, the man who raised me from as far as back as I can remember walked close to my face and began yelling.

"Where is she? Where the fuck is she Lauren? You better tell me where she is. I'll kill that bitch." He didn't look like my father, but a man enraged. I was so scared I started crying helplessly. That didn't stop him from holding me firmly by my shoulders.

"Where the fuck is she Lauren? Tell me now. She's a lying bitch and will pay me for her lies." He continued his angry rant.

"Let me go. I'm not telling you shit dad." I broke free and ran out to my car. He was screaming behind me making my hand shake as I hit the unlock button. I jumped in and without warning my father dropped to his knees and started crying, begging me to stay. I turned the BMW on and hit the gas. I was confused as shit and couldn't believe my father's arrogance. Without thinking I drove to Arnold's office, jumped out, and walked in quickly. His receptionist wasn't at her desk, so I walked toward his office.

There were voices coming from the room so I stopped to listen before entering. What I heard made me freeze in my steps. A very familiar female voice spoke with irritation.

"But of all the women to fuck around with you choose her spoiled ass." The woman's voice was asking.

"I was weak. I will end it right away," Arnold responded.

"I mean it Arnold. The next time I won't be so nice about shit. It's bad enough you're fucking my sister."

"Relax Shannon, I will handle it. You know how I feel about you honey." I couldn't believe my ears.

"Excuse me, may I help you?" Arnold's assistant asked from behind me.

"I wanted to speak to Mr. Blake, but it appears he has a visitor already," I responded, turning to face her.

"Would you like for me to leave him a message?" she asked politely.

"Tell him the bitch who knows his secrets came by." I strutted out of the building in disbelief. Not only was his trifling ass fucking me, but also his sister in law, my father's woman no less. I searched around for my mother's number and dialed it before pulling off. She answered on the second ring.

"Hello."

"Mom?" I asked

"Lauren? It's me. I'm so happy you called."

"Listen, I need to see you." I spoke into the receiver.

"I'm at the church," she responded. I told her I was on my way before disconnecting the call. Someone needs to pay for the shit that's happening to me.

The Waiting Game
Tori

I had nothing else planned for the rest of my day and it felt like the time slowed down after I gave Misha her gifts with the appointment. Since I was already dressed, I decided to drive over to TWO Urban Licks restaurant to take my mind off things. I loved their food, but also the live music. It wasn't crowded during the week so getting a seat was easy. After taking my seat, I shot Misha an 'I miss you' text before placing my order. Eating alone wasn't for me, but I needed the time to clear my head. A group of beautiful women came into the restaurant, all dressed to impress with bright colors and fancy stilettos. I stared at them with admiration, there is nothing like a beautiful black woman with all of their curves, beautiful skin tones, and vibrant attitudes. One of the women waved in my direction breaking me from my trance like gaze.

I waved back and went back to sipping my water until the waitress came with my glass of wine. After lunch I got back into my car and decided to stop by my mom's house. I took the long way around Misha's mom's house to see if the car she was driving was parked out front, but it wasn't. A bit disappointed I headed in the direction of my mom's until I spotted Misha driving by me. I honked the horn twice to get her attention. She slowed down beside my car. I rolled down my window. I could tell she was crying.

"Are you ok?" I asked though I knew my wife well enough to know she wasn't.

"Yeah, I'm fine," she answered.

"Were you crying?" I asked a bit broken.

"I'm fine. Are you headed over to your mom's house?" she changed the subject.

"Yeah," I answered.

"Oh ok, well tell her I said hello." She started to roll up her window.

"Hey Mish!" I yelled out. She turned to look at me once more.

"Yeah." She looked my way and I wanted to take her home and give it to her.

"Are you hungry?" I wasn't trying to act normal, but I wasn't going to give up trying and she knew that about me.

"Yes, but I'm celebrating with Vivian," she answered.

"Celebrating?" I asked curiously.

"I just got a job." She put her head up and her chest back like she was trying to convince herself to be brave. A job, she was making things final which meant my time was running out. I turned my car off and got out. I walked over to her car and leaned down.

"Congratulations Misha, I'm proud of you." I meant what I said, but it hurt to know she was trying to move on. My lips met her forehead.

"Tori, please stop ok. I can't take this. You made your damn decision ok, so go live with it." She was still hurt and this was my fault.

"I know it is and I'm not trying to pressure you, but I swear I miss you. Please tell Vivian you'll catch up with her later," I begged.

"Why? So we can act like we're normal?" She pointed back and forth at each of us.

"We have a lot of shit that needs to be worked on, but the point is we need to work on them. I'm telling you I don't want to walk away."

"So what does that mean because you don't want to I should listen? When I didn't want to did that stop you from ignoring me? Did it stop you from giving me my clothes, changing the locks to the house? Did it even stop you from sleeping with Lauren? No, so please move because I have to go." She pushed my arms away from her car and drove off into the direction of her mom's house.

I was pissed as shit, but I really couldn't say anything because she was right. I could feel the loss of that $120 dollars for the marriage counselor, but I was going to show up to confess my sins and be done with it. I hopped back in my car and drove to my mom's house. I knew she was there when I saw her living room light on. I just hoped she could give me some words of wisdom to stop the mounting stress wrapping around my chest and closing in on me.

"Mama, you here?" I asked loudly.

"Yeah, I'm in here," her voice came from the living room. She was sitting on the couch watching one of her shows.

"How you doing baby?" I kissed her on the forehead before sitting beside her.

"Not so good."

"Oh really, why?" She turned to face me.

"I think I lost her for real this time. She can't see past my sins and more because of how I handled her when she wanted to apologize about the adoption thing. I feel stressed out and really don't know what to do." I told the only woman who would tell me the truth without sugar coating it.

"Well Tori, I can't say I blame her. You slept with her best friend and even in your darkest hour that should've been a forbidden fruit you walked away from. Where she was wrong in not telling you about your child being placed up for adoption it was a sacrifice she made to protect you. She lost a son, as well you sleeping with her best friend was for carnal reasons. You have to make a grand gesture, pray on it then leave it with the Lord." My mom's words hurt, but it was true.

"I made an appointment with a marriage counselor and gave Misha the appointment time for tomorrow. I only hope she shows up." I rubbed my face to distract from my wanting to cry.

My mom talked to me some more before cutting me a slice of her famous sock it to me cake. I had a lot to think about.

After my visit, I drove home listening to the radio when John Legend's song, "This time" came on. He really knew what the hell he was talking about. My house was empty when I got there as it has been for the last few days. I didn't feel like being alone, so I called my boy Marcus and told him to come over to watch a few games. He knew Misha and I were having problems, but he didn't know I slept with Lauren. It took him a half hour to get to my house.

"Hey man." We shook hands and did a quick shoulder tap before he flopped on the couch.

"You want a beer?" I asked.

"Sure, you have Corona?" He asked with his eyes on the television screen.

I went in the kitchen and grabbed two coronas before heading back to sit on the couch.

"Who's playing?" he asked.

"Not really sure, I think a few college teams are on now."

"Misha ain't gone come down stairs tripping is she?" he asked seriously. Misha didn't take to Marcus to much from when we were kids. He used to be a trouble maker, but has calmed down since growing up. Misha didn't see it like that though.

"She moved in with her moms." I took a swig of my beer.

"What?" Surprise registered across his face. For the second time since coming in the house he looked at me.

"Yeah man. A few things took place that fucked up my marriage," I confessed. I told him about the adoption and how Misha found out about me sleeping with Lauren. He sat there with his mouth half open.

"Damn T, that's some fucked up shit."

"Yeah man, but the messed up part about it is I don't want to lose Misha. You know how much I care about her. You remember how hard I worked to get her."

"All you can do is let her know how sorry you are man, but if she don't come around you have to move on. Lauren is a bad bitch though so I ain't mad at you, ya feel me? Yo no offense, but Misha is crazy as hell climbing walls and shit," he tried to laugh it off, but I wasn't feeling it.

"That shit ain't funny."

"I know, my bad. But you know how your wife is, so you can't appeal to her romantic side, but go after her hardcore. You can't get her back on some punk flowers and candy shit. You have to shake her up and say you're my woman dammit." Marcus shook the air like he was holding Misha by the shoulders. He was a fool, but he had a point.

"You're right man. You know what? You gotta go. I'm about to head over there right now." Marcus refueled my inner energy and gave me a crazy insane idea. Misha didn't sit around waiting for me to hear her out, but came after me until her point was heard. I grabbed my wallet and my keys and walked out to my car. My watch read ten thirty so I hoped she was home by now.

Sign from God?
Misha

Seeing Tori earlier messed up my happy mood. I told Vivian what he did and she offered no solutions. For once I wanted to forget about Tori, Lauren, divorce and everything else that reminded me of the last few months. I had a damn job which meant I could move into my own place sooner. After dinner I dropped Vivian off and like before she hugged me tight and asked me to call her if I needed anything. I drove off and debated on stopping at a bar before going home. It was getting late so I decided to just go home. I seemed to catch all of the red lights tonight. At a particularly long red light I stopped to send up a prayer about my marriage.

"Lord, please guide me in the right direction. If it's time to walk away, show me clearly. But if I should stay and fight for my marriage, I need a clear sign." My prayer ended just as the light turned green.

Turning onto my mother's block I noticed a big commotion outside of her door. I squinted to get a good look, but saw Tori's car parked in front of the door. As quick as I could I jumped out of the car and grabbed my purse, my brother Jerry was standing on the porch yelling at Tori.

"She ain't here like I said," Jerry yelled across the yard.

"Tori, what are you doing?" I screamed at him. His eyes lit up when he saw me.

"I came to get my wife," he spoke directly at me. In an instant my knees felt weak.

"What?" I asked instead.

"You heard me Misha. I came to get my wife." He took me by my arm and walked toward his car.

"Wait, where are you taking me?" I pulled away from him.

"Yo, look Tori, get the fuck off my sister dude." Jerry charged off the porch.

"This don't have anything to do with you Jerry." Tori held on to my arm as he yelled at my brother.

With little notice Jerry was charging after Tori. My brother is much shorter and lighter than Tori, but he had the heart of a lion. He swung at Tori's mid-section landing a few blows. My mom was on the porch holding her bible and praying. I ran on the porch and told her to go inside of the house.

"Mama, please I'll handle it ok. Please go inside," I begged her to go inside. She did what I said but stayed in the doorway.

I ran back over to the two.

"Tori stop!" I yelled at his back as he swung punches at my brother's chest and shoulders.

"Tori, I said stop." I reached for his arm and he turned to face me. In that moment Jerry landed a punch to his temple.

"Shit!" Tori yelled out. He stood up ready to kick my brother, but looked at me with intensity.

"I came here to get my damn wife and if that means beating the ass of anyone in my way so be it." He spoke holding his temple. Jerry was still lying on the ground. Tori reached for my arm again and walked me toward his car. I sat down in the passenger side staring at my brother on the ground as Tori came to the driver's side and pulled off.

I wanted my husband in that moment, but I kept quiet as he drove us back to our house. A few blocks away I asked.

"What are you trying to prove?"

"You'll find out soon enough," he answered. When the car reached the driveway. He jumped out and jogged over to my side where he opened the door and picked me up the same as our first day moving into the house. I didn't give him much fight because my body was screaming for him louder than a fire engine. He unlocked the door and carried me directly up to the bedroom where he laid me down across the bed. Tori removed my heels one by one and gently, but eagerly pulled away my skirt. His fingers tugged at my black panties until they were falling to the floor. I held my breath as he stood over me staring at my wetness for a moment. Within seconds he was on his knees licking hungrily at my pussy. Moans escaped my throat and the sensation of his tongue exploring my sex caused me to grip the comforter beneath me.

Tori was my first and only so I had no one else to compare him to, but that never stopped him from working his magic each time we were in the bedroom. He began to strip away his clothes until I could feel his skin against my inner thigh. He stood up to remove his pants. My desire eclipsed my better judgment. For a fleeting moment I felt like I should stand up and bolt out of the room or as if I should use him until I reached a climax and never look back. I thought of my prayer and the fact that less than thirty minutes later I was in the house I once called home being pleasured by Tori.

"Damn, I've missed you Misha," he whispered before lying on his back and pulling me on top of him.

I pushed away any negative thoughts as lust overcame me. I pushed down onto my husband's hardness and moved in slow circles until he grabbed me by the waist. I allowed my hands to glide across his hard chest. I let myself go, giving him all of my desire, all of my pain all of my hurt with each move of my hips. I rode us both into multiple orgasms. With my body spent I dropped down on top of him. Tori wrapped his arms around me for what felt like forever.

"Stay with me tonight," he requested.

"This changes nothing," I whispered back.

"You're right, it changes everything," he answered. I relaxed into him. I didn't have the energy to fight back tonight.

I Pay? No You Pay!
Lauren

I met my mother at her house and told her how my father reacted. She didn't want to tell Joe, but I told her that I was really worried about her safety. Joe threatened his brother, my father's life leaving me with mixed emotions. I left her house feeling like I wanted to hurt someone. Now that I took care of my mother I was out to get Shannon's ass. She tried to kill me to teach Arnold a lesson and now they both would pay. I drove back over to my house to change my clothes. Everything looked the same as I left it, I took a quick shower, slipped on a pair of black tights, my black hoodie and black and white low top adidas. Misha's ass wasn't the only one crazy enough to climb fences. A plan was formulating in my brain. It would be risky, but I was willing to risk it all to watch them both pay.

I took a few deep breaths before texting Arnold telling him that I needed to give it to him badly. I told him that I would be waiting for him at the Econolodge in about an hour. He sent me his usual I'll be there message two seconds later, which let me know she wasn't close by. I waited a good ten minutes before I sent a text to the number that threatened me earlier. I knew it was Shannon and I would now be hosting the night's events. My text read: "I am not afraid of you and I'm not leaving him alone. He is eating my pussy at the Econolodge that he paid for tonight and there isn't anything you can do about it. If you had any balls you would come take care of your business like an adult."

I waited for a response, but it didn't come right away so I headed toward the car. My plan was starting to work out. I didn't give her an address which would force her to have to spend time looking. I called the Econolodge and made a one night reservation and paid for it with the credit card Arnold gave me to use for emergencies. I was going to head over to the hotel and wait for Arnold to arrive in the room I reserved. She must have had me twisted if she thought I was going to take her setting my club on fire on the chin. I've done some questionable shit in my life, but I've never tried to kill anyone.

I pulled into the parking lot, ran into the lobby, and asked for my keys and told the receptionist that if anyone came looking for me it was ok to give them my room number. She nodded her head in agreement and I was off. I needed to at least have the television lights on so Arnold wouldn't be suspicious. I put on the gloves I placed in my hoodie pockets before opening the door. I used a towel to leave the door slightly open and checked my cell for the time. There was a message from the same mysterious number. It read: We'll see about that. Good she got the message. I knew he would be on his way and that Shannon must be with my dad, looking desperately for a way out of the house.

I sent Tori an 'I miss you, I really do love you' text and crossed my fingers that he would see that his life was better with me than without me. After setting up the scene I walked back over to my rental car a few parking spots down from the room. I checked the area with no sign of Arnold anywhere. I thought Shannon may have diverted his attention by side tracking him but then again every woman would rather catch her man in the act. Misha taught me that. When I started to get restless I noticed headlights behind my car slowing down a few spots beside me. I laid my head back on the headrest to avoid someone seeing me. It was Arnold jumping out of his car and walking carelessly over to the hotel room. I wasn't worried about his leaving. He stepped in cautiously because the door was left opened, but walked in. I left him a note on the bed saying I went to get something for us to drink, but would be back shortly. One of my sexy night gowns were left on the bed for affect.

I spotted another car coming up and parked a few spots to Arnold's right. Once I was sure it was Shannon I sent my dad a text telling him my mom was at the Econolodge and I gave him the room number. I knew he would break his neck trying to get here. If he took the highway he could be here in less than fifteen minutes. I turned to see Shannon looking around the parking lot. Then she tip toed up to the window and began trying to look through the curtains. I didn't think she was going to knock at first, but then I saw her texting a message on her phone. She calmly waited for the person to text her back which took a few minutes before she looked down at her phone again. She continued to wait, which surprised me. I expected her to try to kick the door down, but she didn't. Then out of know where she knocked on the door. I rolled my window down to hear. Arnold opened the door.

"What you forgot your key baby?" He was asking, but his face froze when he saw Shannon standing on the other side. He tried to close the door but she pushed it open forcefully.

"Oh really, Arnold? Where is she?" He was stammering uncontrollably. I've never seen him look so uncomposed.

Don't worry Arnold she has what's coming to her, I thought to myself. Just like clock-work my father's car came to a screeching halt as he slammed on his brakes. The room door was still open when he got out looking like a mad man. He charged into the room and stopped without warning. I could only see his back, but his words were loud and clear.

"What the fuck?"

With great care I eased my car door open and slid out quietly. I needed to get closer to see what was going on. Crouching low, I crept a few cars down until I was in line with the door. Shannon spun around to see my dad standing there with a look of devastation.

"Yeah, now what do you have to say?" I asked.

"Lauren, this isn't what it looks like," she stammered, but I knew my dad wasn't going to hear any of it.

"Really? Cause it looks like my woman is in a hotel room with another man after she just told me she was going to take care of something work related," he belted out angrily.

"Hold on my man. There's no need to yell at her like that," Arnold stepped up.

"Don't say shit to me." My dad looked in his direction briefly before diverting his attention back to Shannon. She looked stunned, probably how I looked when Misha's crazy ass came into my bedroom.

"Do you have something you want to say to me?" My dad yelled at her.

"Listen Lauren, I, I..." she stuttered because she couldn't come up with any logical or acceptable explanation for why she was there.

I was glad my dad was there to handle her ass though I knew he would chew me out after finding out I lied about my mom being there. I didn't care because the way I see it he still owes me an explanation. I saw him reach behind his back and pull out a black object. He pointed it toward both Arnold and Shannon, making Shannon scream and cry. Arnold raised his hands up like you do when the cops tell you too. My heart pounded through my chest. I only wanted them to get caught not killed.

Shit! I said under my breath.

If I go to the door, they will all know I set this up and God only knows how that will play out or I could sit quietly and let my dad do something crazy and spend the rest of his days behind bars. That may not be a bad idea if it means my mom is safe. The room door closed and it made me panic. I jogged over to the window, looking around to be sure no one was out watching from nearby. The coast was clear. I could hear my dad yelling at them both to get on their knees with their hands in the air.

'He's going to execute them,' I couldn't help thinking it, but then I remembered that Shannon tried to burn me alive and I strutted to my car and got in. They were all adults and if she thought I was going to be the only one paying for this I said to hell with that, she pays.

An Almost Perfect Night
Tori

Misha and I made love two more times before she finally fell asleep. I felt like there was a small bit of hope left for us. I got up to relieve myself and then headed downstairs into the kitchen for something to drink. I noticed my cell phone light flashing on the couch so I grabbed it on my way to the kitchen. I had a message from Lauren, telling me that she loved me and missed me. I exited out of messages and placed the phone on the kitchen counter. I needed to change my number in the morning. I felt sweaty and smelled of sex, but it made me smile. Misha dominated in the bedroom which was real new. After guzzling down a bottled water, I turned off the light and headed back upstairs. Misha was still knocked out like a champ. I slid into bed beside her and wrapped my arms around her, I couldn't remember the last time I was at this much peace.

Misha started moving making me turn around in my sleep. That's when I heard a loud banging downstairs.

"Tori, what is that?" Misha asked with a groggy voice.

"What?" I asked still half asleep until I heard it again. It sounded like someone was banging on the door. I pulled the covers back and ran down the steps quickly. Nobody ever came to my house this late.

"Who is it?" I asked close to the heavy wooden door.

"It's Lauren, open the door please it's important." Lauren spoke through the door.

"Shit," I said under my breath. I looked over my shoulder to the stairs to make sure Misha wasn't standing in the hallway. It was clear.

"Now is really not a good time." My heart was pounding.

"Open the damn door Tori, NOW!" Lauren started to scream. I didn't know what to do, but I swear I felt like knocking her ass out. I quietly turned the lock. Begging God to let Misha stay in a deep sleep long enough for me to kick Lauren out.

"What?" I asked. She was wearing all black except for her sneakers.

"Did you get my text?" she asked seductively. I couldn't believe this. Of all the nights she wanted to show up it had to be the night Misha finally agreed to stay.

"No, listen it really isn't a good time." I tried to remain calm to keep her from elevating her voice.

"Why? I had some crazy shit go down tonight and I really need someone to talk to about it." She looked anxious.

"Who is that Tori?" Misha's voice came from the top of the stairs. My heart dropped down to the soles of my feet. Lauren's face froze in disbelief.

"You have Misha here?" she asked with fire behind her eyes.

"Move." Misha was behind me now. I swear I didn't even hear her come down the steps. Before I could pull her away, she was pushing the door open wider.

"I was patient with your ass, but I see you really trying to get your ass beat." She lunged at Lauren, grabbing her by the hair and pulling it hard. With her head being pulled low, Lauren tried to grab for Misha, but couldn't reach. Misha was kneeing her in the face. I grabbed her by the waist and pulled her back but she wouldn't let Lauren's hair go.

"Let her go. I'm going to handle this," I yelled.

"Get off my hair! Get the fuck off my hair bitch!" Lauren was yelling pass me. Finally Misha let go with my hands prying her fingers loose.

Now free, Lauren tried hard to hit Misha in the face, but I held her back with one arm.

"Listen Lauren, I'm going to say this only one more time. We were in the wrong and we can't be together. I want it to work with Misha and I really need you to respect that." I looked her in the face and saw her heart breaking behind her eyes. I turned to Misha and she puffed her chest out victoriously.

"You know what Tori? If you want her broke down ass, you deserve her. I gave you everything you were missing," Lauren's voice cracked. I felt bad that things got this far, but Misha has been ride or die. I felt my wife revving up to swing, but it was too late for me to stop it. She landed a powerful blow to Lauren's chest that knocked her backwards and on her ass.

"You trifling ass bitch. You think you gone come over here disrespecting me to my damn face? I don't think so. You can go around fucking other people's husbands all you want, but I'll be damned if you gone talk shit to me in my face. Now go call your daddy to come rescue your dumb ass like you always do." Misha stood over her for a moment longer than necessary and walked back in the house.

"Close the door Tori." She demanded over her shoulder. I felt sorry for Lauren, but I closed the door and locked it.

When I walked into the living room, Misha was standing by the fireplace.

"Look, I'm not going to keep going through this shit ok? Tonight was a mistake, I shouldn't have let you bring me here. You have unresolved feelings." She started, but I cut her off.

"Misha, there is nothing unresolved."

"Yes the fuck it is Tori. Her ass thinks she can keep coming over here unannounced like she got it like that. Obviously, I was so horrible that she was filling in gaps that you felt you had," she continued.

"This won't happen again, I promise."

"Is that before or after she flatten all your tires," Misha spoke with her face toward the window.

"What?" I ran over to the window and saw Lauren standing by my car. I couldn't believe this nonsense. I ran back to the front door.

"What the hell are you doing?" I shouted at her. With Tears in her eyes, Lauren picked up a brick from my garden and raised it above her head.

"Listen, if you throw that brick so help me God." I wasn't about to have this go down. I used my car for work.

"I'm tired of this Tori, I don't have nobody and I thought I had you. I loved you on purpose and now I'm losing you," she spoke through tears.

"This whole situation is messed up Lauren. I didn't mean for it to go this damn far, ok? I didn't mean to hurt you or Misha, but it has to end somewhere. You breaking my car windows ain't gone fix anything." I tried reasoning with her. She still had her hand raised. I walked slowly in her direction, my eyes focusing on the brick in her hand. "I thought we had something, I don't go around fucking with dudes for no damn reason." Lauren continued her helpless rant. Misha stood by the door listening.

"I'm calling a damn cab, I don't have time for this desperate bitch. You have everything Lauren. Why the fuck did you need my little piece of a life?" Misha shouted.

I need to get Lauren out of here fast. I didn't need Misha trying to leave.

"Misha get in the house. You're not going anywhere. Lauren, I said I'm sorry. We wouldn't have made it anyway." I tried to speak calmly, but Misha started yelling again.

"You don't owe her ass an explanation. She is a trifling ass whore who fucks dudes for status. She thinks she is so different, but the reality is you're a well-paid prostitute."

"Misha get in the house NOW and close the damn door. I said I will handle it!" I yelled at Misha, but she was going to provoke Lauren into messing up my whip and I couldn't have that. I turned to stare at my wife until she did what I said. A few dogs were barking from the commotion.

"Look me in the eye Tori and tell me you don't love me and I'll leave you alone for good." The brick dropped in the yard as she stared at me for an answer. I thought it would be easy. I waked over to Lauren and looked down into her eyes. She looked crazy, but was still beautiful. Hurt registered on her face and like a flash of light my memory served me all of the moments she was there making me feel good. Lauren never made me feel low, but actually made me feel like a boss. The words caught in my throat, I could feel Misha's eyes burning through my back.

"In another life you would have been perfect for me, but I can't love you right now. I can't give you my heart because it already belongs to her." The words came out a little above a whisper. She dropped her shoulders and walked in the direction of the silver BMW parked on the curb.

I thought I would feel relieved to see her leave, but I felt like shit for hurting a woman who really did try her hardest to give me what I thought I wanted. *'Damn man,'* I thought to myself, I only hoped she'd be able to forgive me. I walked back in the house and saw Misha putting her shoes on.

"Where are you goin?" I asked confused.

"Tori, I feel like I am capable of doing anything if that bitch comes here again. Whatever the fuck you did to her has her whipped."

"Misha, come on we were just making love." She cut me off.

"You're right and it was almost a good night. I'm a lot of things, but I'm not desperate or stupid ok? I love you

Tori, but I love myself more." She was ranting as she looked around for her cell phone.

"What are you going to do take a cab?" I asked.

"Yes or call Jerry to come get me."

"I'll drive you back home." I wasn't going to have her getting in a cab in the middle of the night.

"Fine." She huffed and flopped down on the couch.

"After the appointment." I ran over to the couch and playfully tackled her.

"We are beyond counseling, get off of me." She laughed, so I knew she wasn't as angry.

"Come on babe, you can't give me what you gave me upstairs and still say you ready to walk out." I was being serious.

"Every time I want to consider working it out, Lauren's trifling ass comes over. Maybe it's a sign that we should move on. I'm not competing with an entitled bitch. The funny thing is once you're divorced she won't even want your ass anymore. She only wants what she thinks she can't have. I was her friend Tori, I know her hustle. The bitch don't even have a personality because she changes into whatever her man wants. Your ass was conned, you fell for it, and for as long as I'm here fighting for you she'll want you. But as soon as the ink hits the divorce papers, like smoke she'll disappear." Her words left me silent, as we lay on the couch looking up at the ceiling I started remembering all of the stories Misha told me about Lauren using dudes, making them buy her things more expensive than a six figure mortgage. It started making me angry the more I thought about it, but I wouldn't let Misha know it.

I wrapped my arms around her slowly to test her resistance. She didn't fight, but let me pull her into me. I really wanted another chance with my wife. She was feisty as hell, but she always kept it real.

"I wished I would have never fucked with her. I swear I was lonely, I missed you Misha believe it or not and she gave me the attention I wanted from you," I told the truth.

"Tori, I'm sorry for what I did with our son. I should have come to you and let you make a decision, but I knew you would want to keep the baby and would have dropped out of school. I wasn't about to be the one who ruined your life."

"We don't have to talk about that anymore. I know why you did it," I squeezed her.

"I can't get over Lauren though. Of all the bitches in the world you picked her to do your dirt with."

"Mish." I tried to stop her. There was only one direction this conversation could go.

"No, let me finish. You know I met Lauren when we were like eighteen right? She was always so spoiled, but what I liked about her was her ambition. I knew she wouldn't stop till she ruled the world. I lived through her in a way. She used to want to come around me and my mom all the time and my mom actually treated her like a daughter. I knew she was jealous because my mom was around." I felt Misha trembling as she spoke which let me know she was crying.

'Shit,' I thought to myself. All I could do was hold her, but I felt like crap. I held her until we both fell asleep.

Time to Let Go
Misha

I woke up before sunrise on the couch with Tori, I stood up slowly, so he wouldn't know I left. I walked upstairs to grab my purse and cell phone so I could leave. It felt good to have sex with Tori and I almost believed my prayer was answered when I saw him at my mom's but then Lauren showed up and let me know I was tripping. For as long as she knew I wanted him she wouldn't give him peace and before I went off the deep end and spent life in prison for a heinous, vicious act of violence, I'd rather walk away.

I called a cab from the curb in front of the house and waited for them to arrive. I know he thought I was going to come to his appointment but I needed time to think it through. If I went it would be to seek closure for myself before going to our divorce hearing. Once the cab arrived I gave him my mom's address and laid my head back on the headrest. I've had more drama in the last few weeks than I've had in the whole time we were married. There was one things I knew for sure, if I knew my husband I knew he wouldn't give up, just like when we were teenagers he harassed me into a yes I'd be his girl. I smiled to myself thinking about it.

I remember when Lauren and Tori first met she said he was to skinny and that he didn't look like he was going to be much, but the more time I spent with him the more I saw his potential. I gave the cab driver a twenty dollar bill and stepped out of the car. The streets were quiet with only a few people getting in their cars to head off to work. I waved at my mom's neighbor sitting out on the porch. My mom was sitting in the living room drinking a cup of coffee. I kissed her forehead.

"Sorry about last night," I apologized.

"It's ok, I didn't expect anything less coming from Tori. He's always been a persistent one." She took a sip from her cup. I flopped beside her on the couch.

"Ain't that the truth?" I agreed.

"I was sitting her thinking about how he would come around looking for you and your brother's would all stand outside watching him," she laughed, which made me smile.

"Mama, I really feel lost. He made an appointment with a marriage counselor for today. I don't think I can forget about what he did with Lauren. She came around last night trying to tell him that she wants to be with him." I rested my head on her shoulder. My mom tensed up for a moment before speaking.

"That child was always looking for love. A man can only love a woman child from a fatherly perspective, but she needed a mother's love to show her balance, compassion, and integrity. I pray that Lauren can see the error of her ways before it's too late." My mother was always praying for someone, but all I wanted to do was bash her head in.

"Are you going to go?" she asked.

"I'm not sure. I love Tori and I can forgive him, but I can't forget what I saw. And I know I probably don't have a right to talk after what I've done, but my intention wasn't to hurt him. I didn't do it out of spite."

"Well baby, the way I see it, you were both wrong and if he is willing to work pass your transgression then you should consider working pass his, after you make him sweat of course. Now let me go start breakfast." She kissed my head and stood to go into the kitchen. I pulled myself up and shuffled up the stairs to take a shower. The smell of Tori still lingered on my skin. My phone started buzzing with messages from him asking why I left. I told him I needed time to think. With the warm water running in the tub, I dialed Arnold's office to ask a question, but was told by his receptionist he hadn't arrived yet. I left him a message to call me when he got in and hung up. My shower was longer than most. I tried to forget Tori's touch, his scent. I needed to erase last night from my mind.

After my shower, I changed into a pair of yoga pants and a t-shirt and went back down for breakfast. My mom was chatting away on the phone as she handed me a plate of food. Jerry came down a few minutes later.

"Good morning," I threw over my shoulder.

"Whatever," he answered.

"What's wrong with you?" I stopped eating and turned to face him.

"Hmmmm, let's see, it may have something to do with me protecting you and then you getting into Tori's car with me lying on the ground," Jerry answered sarcastically.

"I'm sorry Jerry, I was just trying to calm the situation."

"Then you should have brought your ass in the house and locked the door," he responded, "Sorry mama," he said to my mom for cursing.

"I said I was sorry. I'm not going to repeat it or go around kissing your butt ok?" Jerry was getting on my nerves. It wasn't like I wanted my brother to get hurt, but I also didn't want to see him and Tori going at it all night.

"Why you not at work anyway?" I asked

"I'm on my way after breakfast. You better tell him not to come around here disrespecting my mom's house no more," Jerry threatened.

"Jerry hush up. Your sister is dealing with some things, ok?" My mother interjected, reminding me of when we were kids.

"You lucky your mom is here," he teased before sitting down to eat. Jerry was the only kid to never move out of mama's house. He was twenty two and decided college wasn't for him, so he got a job instead. His favorite line is, 'Girls my age don't care about all that.' I had to agree because he always had a girl running after him wanting to know where he was or what he was doing.

He left for work and I spent a few hours watching television and talking with my mom before taking a nap. The day was going by quickly and three o'clock was fast approaching. I needed to make up my mind about going to the counselor and Tori already sent me a few messages asking was I coming. I went through my closet for something sexy to wear. I wanted to him to regret his decision, every time he saw me. I spotted a form fitting black maxi dress that enhanced my curves. I curled my hair until it surrounded my face perfectly, did my makeup and picked out a pair of sexy pink and black stilettos. On my way out of the room, I spotted the tiffany gift bag Tori gave me and I put on the beautiful diamond bracelet he just got me.

I told my mom I'd be back as I headed to my rental car. I had only twenty minutes to get to the appointment so I drove over to the address on the card. I took my time, taking the long route. I didn't want to get their before Tori.

Picking Sides
Lauren

To say I was devastated about Tori choosing Misha would be an understatement. A few weeks ago I would have bet all I had that he would have walked away with me. After leaving his house I drove to our favorite quickie spot in the park behind the bushes and trees. I eventually fell asleep in my car. This wasn't me, I am Lauren Michaels, every man's fantasy. I caused pain not received it. The sunlight poured in my car windows making me cover my eyes. Today was the last day I made a fool out of myself for Tori or any other man for that matter.

The image of Arnold and Shannon being held by gun point made me wake up completely. I pulled out my cell phone and dialed Arnold's office.

"Hello. You've reached the office of Mr. Blake," his receptionist answered.

"Hi, I need to speak with Mr. Blake, it's urgent." My words came out rushed.

"I'm sorry ma'am he hasn't come in yet. Would you like to leave a message?" I hung up at the end of her question.

'Please God don't say my dad killed them,' I thought to myself. I started the BMW and headed in the direction of my dad's house. I needed to see if his car was there. I caught every traffic light creating more and more anxiety. I finally arrived and my dad's car wasn't parked on the street. I jumped out of the car and ran over to his house. I was too short to see into his garage. I ran over to his front door and banged as hard as I could. There was no answer and I couldn't hear any movement on the other side.

"Dad? Open the door!" I yelled in desperation. His neighbors came out to look at my charade. One even stopped walking his dog to stare at me. I didn't care. He wasn't there, so I ran back to my car and grabbed my cell to dial his number.

I tried three times with no answer. *What the hell?* My mine was racing with tons of scenarios. I made my way over to the hotel. Maybe they were all able to sit down and talk about things rationally I lied to myself. If there was one thing I learned I knew nothing was rational with matters of the heart. Pulling into the hotel parking lot, I spotted yellow caution tape in the section close to the hotel room I paid for last night. Police were telling the small crowd of onlookers to move back. I pulled into a parking space and jumped out, running over to the area with all the people. The door to the hotel room was open and I spotted Arnold standing by the door talking to one of the police. Good he was alive. My father was lying on a gurney close to an ambulance. I ran over to him.

"Dad?"

"Lauren." He turned his head to face me. I didn't understand what was happening. I couldn't see Shannon and my dad had blood on his shoulder.

"What happened?" I asked with fear coursing through my veins.

"I need you to go home and wait for my call." My dad instructed me. I didn't want to believe that he may have done something violently stupid. I just wanted her to learn her lesson. Tears began welling in my eyes. There was a knocking sound coming from behind a glass. I turned to face a patrol car, my uncle Joe was sitting in the back of a squad car. My mouth dropped, I turned to face my father again. This time I looked closely at the blood on his shirt and it was accompanied by a bullet hole.

"He shot you?" I asked in disbelief. My dad grabbed me by the wrist.

"I need you to go home and wait for me to call you." He stared me directly in the eyes. What was happening?

"Dad tell me what happened?" I begged. Arnold saw me and called me over to him.

"Arnold is here." My dad looked in his direction.

"Don't trust his ass Lauren, listen to me. Will you do what I said? I need you to trust me." I ripped my arm away from him when the realization of what he intended to do flooded me all at once. He came to that hotel with the intent on killing my mother.

I walked over to Arnold.

"What happened to you last night?" he asked with curiosity.

"I left to get something for us to drink and spotted Shannon's car in the parking lot, so I left," I lied.

"She, she was," he tried to lie, but I cut him off.

"I don't give a damn why she was here. Did you know she set my club on fire?" I looked him in the eye, but he looked away which spoke volumes.

"Listen, Lauren I don't know how to say this," he started off.

"Save it, I heard enough from you and Shannon back at your office yesterday." His eyes grew wide.

"I want you to sign the papers giving me full ownership of Club Seduction. Your wife and her crazy ass sister can have your ass and if I were you I'd tell Shannon to get her a good criminal attorney." I walked away with both Arnold and my dad calling after me.

I needed to see my mom to fully understand what happened. I fought back tears as I made my way back to her house. She answered the door after my third knock. Worry registered across her face. I stepped into the hall and gave her a hug, we both stood crying in each other's arms like something off of the color purple.

"Joe didn't come home last night," she said as we walked into the living room.

"Mom, I hate to tell you this, but I just saw Joe sitting in the back of a police car." I looked at my hands when I gave her the news. She put her hand to her mouth and started crying again.

"Oh my God no. He didn't do it?" she asked a rhetorical question.

"I need to know what happened." I told her, not really sure if I wanted to know.

"After you told us how angry your father was, Joe called up a friend of his who is a private detective. He had his friend find your dad and to follow him. It took him a few hours to locate his house and from there he followed your dad. Joe received a call saying your dad left the house and went over to a hotel, so Joe left and I haven't heard anything from him until you just came." I couldn't believe this. My dad went to the hotel to kill both my mom and his brother and my uncle went to the hotel to kill my dad. All while Shannon went to the hotel to confront and or hurt me and Arnold. All of this shit started from Misha walking in on me and Tori and I wished I could take it all back, especially now knowing that Tori's ass would turn on me. The only good thing to come from all this is finding my mom.

    I walked over to the love seat and sat next to my mom and laid my head in her lap. I was tired of everything. She stroked my hair as I cried into her dress.

    "He wants me to go home and wait for his call," I spoke through tears.

    "Who?" she asked confused.

    "My dad. I can't even look at him anymore. I don't have anyone left." I cried uncontrollably.

    "That's where you're wrong, you have me." She squeezed my arm.

"I don't think you're safe. Joe is probably going to be arrested and if my dad finds you he may try to hurt you."

"Don't worry about me."

My cell phone buzzed in the same moment she said that. It was my dad asking me where I was. He said he just made it to the hospital and that he needed me. I ignored his message and tried to calm myself down enough to think clearly. I was literally being forced to pick a side, the mother I just met after all of these years over the father who raped and kidnapped me from my mother.

Lay it all on the Table
Tori

I was the first to arrive to the counselor's office. The receptionist told me to wait until the doctor finishes up a few things. My heart beat loudly and I wasn't sure if Misha would actually show up. I played with my hands and thought about what I would want to discuss if she did show up. I knew our problems ran deeper than just my infidelity or even the adoption situation, but I was willing to put them on the table with a mediator in the room if it meant I could have my wife back. Not a lot of my friends liked Misha's sassy attitude, but they all knew she was good for me and kept me on point when we were good. Jazz tunes came from a speaker I couldn't see as I waited. Looking at my watch let me know it was almost five and she wasn't here yet. I had to remember she liked to take her time especially if doing her hair was involved.

A door opened a few feet away and a pretty full figured woman wearing a black skirt, white dress shirt, and black blazer came to the door.

"Mr. Carter?" she asked in my direction. I stood up and followed her into the room.

"Have a seat." She pointed toward a dark brown leather sofa. I sat down slowly, embarrassed to be in marriage counseling alone.

"How are you?" she asked with a polite smile written across her face.

"I'm fine, well under the circumstances I guess." I answered while rubbing my hands together.

"Your form says this will be a couple's session," she started.

"Yeah, I uh, invited my wife Misha to come, but I'm not altogether sure she'll show up. We're facing a divorce," I explained.

"I see, well if you'd like we can start with you." She took her gaze away from the paper and lowered it onto the desk.

"Not sure where to begin." I felt nervous. Like the doctor could see my sins and it didn't help that she was a woman.

"Well let's start with what brought you here today." Her brown eyes pierced right through me.

"To be honest, I wanted to show my wife that I really want our marriage, so I made the appointment to come today," I confessed.

"Ok, that's a good start. What are you saving your marriage from?" She asked a question that would take more than an hour to disclose. I laughed uncomfortably.

"My wife has been…"

"Been what?" Misha's voice came from the doorway.

"Excuse me," the doctor spoke up.

"I'm sorry. I'm Misha Carter, his wife for now." She introduced herself as she walked over to take a seat. She wore the dress that hugged her curves, the heels that made her calves look toned, and the bracelet that put a smile on my face.

"Have a seat. We were just discussing why your husband feels the marriage needs to be saved," the doctor continued.

"I can answer that Dr." Misha looked on the desk for the doctor's name.

"Dr. Masters. My marriage is dying because of my inability to communicate and his infidelity." Misha finished her sentence, causing the doctor to raise an eyebrow.

"I see that you are very sure on that, then I guess Mr. Carter your marriage cannot be saved." Dr. Masters responded a bit sarcastically.

"Wait what?" I asked. I know I didn't spend one hundred and twenty dollars for her to tell me that.

"Your wife seems to have come to a conclusion already." Both the doctor and I turned our attention to Misha.

"I don't have the conclusion. I just stated our problem," Misha confirmed.

"Mrs. Carter the terms you've used for your problems are merely on the surface terms given to avoid digging deeper. Let me ask you a question. Do you still love your husband?"

I dropped my head not sure if I could handle the answer.

"Yes a lot." Misha took a moment before answering that.

"You've said you have an inability to communicate," the doctor continued.

"Yes, I run from discussing issues that are very important," Misha answered.

"Why do you run?"

"Because facing reality hurts," Misha spoke barely above a whisper.

"Let me ask you Mr. Carter. Your wife has said you have been unfaithful in the marriage." The doctor's eyes stared now in my direction.

"Yes, I've slept with one other woman during our relationship." I didn't want to open that can of worms so soon.

"But tell her who with Tori." Like a school girl, Misha turned to face me while folding her hands in her lap.

"Her best friend." I dipped my head low waiting to be ripped apart by both women.

"Do you know what caused you to step out on the marriage?" the doctor asked instead.

I could give a few reasons, but I knew our hour was quickly approaching an end.

"I felt underappreciated and uncared for. I love my wife, but she's treated me cold for a long time. She made me feel like I was less than a man for desiring her. I take Misha for who she is, her attitude, her mouth. I take all of it, but I'm still a man with emotions." I glanced over at Misha and I noticed a tear sliding down her face. I wasn't trying to make her cry, but if I was here I should at least get my money's worth.

"Did you know he felt that way?" the doctor asked Misha.

"No, I admit that I treated him badly. I was going through a few things myself. We suffered two miscarriages and years earlier before we got married I placed our son up for adoption without discussing it with him." It was her turn to lower her head.

I know the doctor was thinking she hit the jackpot with all the problems we have.

"I will give you this Mrs. Carter, there is a communication problem here, but I don't think you're doomed. If the two of you'd like, we can reschedule another appointment for same time next week?" She looked at us both. I was in if she was.

"I'm in." I said. Out of nowhere Misha bolted up from her seat and walked quickly out of the room.

"Excuse me Dr. Masters. Make the appointment." I stood up and excused myself. I didn't want Misha to get in her car before I could talk to her.

When I got outside she was walking toward her car. I thanked God for Stilettos, designed to make a woman walk slow and sexy not fast.

"Misha!" I shouted. She didn't turn around.

"Misha Joyce Carter!" I yelled at her. I knew if I used her middle name she'd stop. She stopped walking, giving me enough time to jog up behind her.

"Why'd you run out?" I asked putting my hands on her hips.

"Because we are fooling ourselves. Our problems are deeper than any marriage counselor can fix," she answered.

"You're right, the doctor can't fix our problems if we're not willing to put in the work." I went to kiss her on the forehead.

"I'll see you at the divorce meeting tomorrow. Bring your lawyer." She pulled away and strutted toward her car. I stood looking like an ass in the middle of the street stunned as hell. I couldn't believe she still wanted to go through with a divorce.

"Why the fuck did you waste my time? Huh? You know what, fine. I will see you tomorrow!" I yelled at her back. If she wants to walk away fine by me, I put it all on the table and if it's not good enough I'm not begging any woman to stay with me.

I was wrong for my part, but it took to fuck up our marriage. I walked over to my car angrily. I couldn't believe this nonsense. I reached for the door without unlocking it and it set off the car alarm. '*She got me twisted,*' I thought to myself. I hit the unlock button on my keys and yanked the door open. I'm not a fool that much she should know. I turned the car on and pulled out of my parking spot. I felt like hitting something, beating the life out of something. She wasted my damn time if she knew she was planning on telling me she'd still see me at the meeting tomorrow.

I drove at top speed in the direction of the nearest bar. Then I remembered Lauren, how sad she looked the other day and I turned a corner to ride over to Club Seduction. '*If she doesn't care about me, why should I care about her?*' I asked myself. When I pulled up to the club there were contractors working on the outside of the building. I walked around back and pounded on the office door. A few seconds later Chris answered.

"Hey man, is Lauren here?" I asked.

"Naw man, she's not, but I'll tell her you stopped by," he answered before closing the door again.

I turned to leave and yelled, "FUCKKKKKK!" at the top of my lungs. There was nothing left to do, but accept defeat and recognize the woman I spent all of my adult life with was no longer mine. I sat in my car for a moment to calm my racing heart before deciding to go to a bar to get wasted.

Mind Made Up
Misha

The truth is, sitting in the office, I realized how much I loved Tori, but also how much I knew I wouldn't be able to deal with him on an intimate level. I heard what he said about how he felt and that's when it hit me. If I was able to keep the adoption from him and treat him like crap, how much more would I start to act like a bitch over knowing he fucked Lauren? I didn't want to turn into the crazy, controlling wife asking him where he was, who he was with. I didn't want to end up like Tasha from, "Why Did I Get Married?" I knew that much about myself and to spare him the trouble of filing for divorce later I'd step back and do it for him now.

When he said fine, he'll see me tomorrow my heart sank. I knew we were over because Tori could hold to a grudge. I got in my car and removed the bracelet he gave me. I placed it in the small pocket in my purse and zipped it shut. Before I could pull off my cell phone rang. I thought it might be Tori, but it was Arnold's office number.

"Hello?" I answered.

"Misha? It's me Arnold." He spoke on the other end.

"Yea, I called you earlier. I just wanted to make sure we were still on tomorrow."

"Yes, sorry to be getting back to you so late," he apologized.

"It's ok, I'm not doing anything."

"Well look, if you don't have anything planned, I'd really like to meet with you. How about dinner? I haven't eaten yet," he suggested. I wondered what he wanted to discuss.

"Ok, where?" I asked.

He gave me the name of an uppity restaurant I've never been to before and told me the directions. I put the address into the rental's gps and headed in that direction. I tried to push me and Tori's relationship to the back of my mind. It was time for me to take care of me. I wanted to start being involved with our son and I needed a clear mind if I wanted to accomplish that. Eventually Tori would move on and find him a woman, he deserved to be with. I pulled up to the parking lot and a valet met me at the door. I gave him my keys and walked toward the door. A hostess wearing a black dress greeted me at the door.

"Party of?" she asked.

"I'm here to meet Arnold Blake," I answered.

"Ah, Mr. Blake is waiting follow me please." She walked away from the podium with me following behind. I was led to a table where Arnold sat drinking a glass of red wine.

"Misha, I'm glad you've made it." He stood up and pulled out my chair.

"Thanks."

I wasn't sure how to take Arnold. He seemed friendly and I knew he was flirtatious because he was seeing Lauren, but I couldn't tell if he was just being nice, so me I told myself to keep my eyes opened. He walked back over to his seat.

"How are you?" he asked

"I'm fine, I guess." Was my response.

"Would you like a glass of wine?" the hostess asked.

"Blackberry Merlot, please." I placed an order.

When she walked away, Arnold sat back in his chair and studied me for a moment longer than I thought necessary.

"Misha, what do you hope to get out of this divorce?" he asked with a smug smile on his face. An expression both me and Tori would have wanted to smack off a few months ago.

"I don't know I was angry before, so I would have said I want it all. Now, I really don't know what I want," I answered honestly. When I walked in Lauren's bedroom and saw her sitting on my husband's lap, I would have made him give me everything he owns and left him with the boxers he wore over to her house. Now, I just feel like I want to just walk away with nothing, just cut my ties.

"Listen, you are in a very good position right now. Georgia is an equitable distribution state so whatever he has obtained during your marriage you are entitled to half." He paused to let that sink in. I really only wanted the car or for him to get me one, so I could have a means of transportation.

"I think I want him to get me a car so I can get back and forth to work and I would also like a small amount of alimony to help me until I get on my feet."

Arnold laughed. "I don't think you hear me. We can take the bastard down for what he's done to you," he elevated his voice and him calling Tori a bastard made me want to jump up and smack him.

"I had time to cool off and feel like I want to only take what I need versus what I want. I'm not trying to destroy him or leave him in the poor house." I dared him to say something smart about Tori again so I could go off on him. Even though, I wasn't sure why it made me mad.

My Merlot came and I took a sip as I read over the menu. Arnold looked a bit upset, but he composed himself.

"I will respect your wishes, but I need you to understand what you have to gain in this situation. Most women in your situation would take him for all he's got and I feel it would be justified," Arnold started but all I heard was hypocrite.

"So should your wife take you for everything?" I asked while putting my glass to my mouth. He stopped and smiled a sinister smile before giving me a 'you got me' head nod.

"Fair enough." He tipped his glass my way. The waitress came and introduced herself and took our orders. I felt like steak and potatoes to go with my Merlot. I needed more time to think things over. Arnold started asking me questions about Lauren and if she was talking to anyone else other than Tori. I let him know I wouldn't be surprised if she was but she only talked about him, which was true.

"I like you Misha. You're very straight forward. It's his loss," Arnold complimented me.

"Thanks, but to be fair we've both committed our sins. I just hate that he chose her. She has it all and the fact that her ass had to have what was mine pisses me off." I was speaking more to myself than him.

"No worries, she has what's coming to her," he confirmed. I didn't dig into it, but he sounded like he had a few things brewing.

We spent another hour discussing my new job, he gave me a few tips on how to handle his partner that I appreciated. I told him I was going to find me my own place and he pulled out a check book and started writing. When he was done, he slid a check over to me.

"Here, take this. I know you'd rather have your place sooner rather than later. Consider it a house warming gift," he said as I looked at the check. The numbers read five thousand five hundred dollars, but my brain was reeling.

"I can't take that." I pushed it back at him.

"You can and you will. I'm not an Indian giver. Get yourself a place, we need your head clear when you come to work and living with your mother is not the best way to obtain that trust me." He laughed it off and I had to talk myself into finishing my meal. If Arnold's ass thought he was getting some, he might want to reconsider his position on that. Unlike Lauren, I wasn't a hoe and I damn sure wasn't selling my goods. I was definitely interested in knowing his angle though.

After dinner he paid the bill and walked me to my car.

"Thanks for dinner and for the check. You'll be the first one I invite to my house warming party." I laughed and hit him on the wrist playfully.

"No problem, I'm sure you deserve it." He leaned forward and kissed me on the cheek.

"Take care of yourself and I'll see you tomorrow." I got into my car feeling awkward and like I did something grimy for accepting this man's money. It almost felt like I cheated on Tori for a moment, but I reminded myself that he was guilty of much more.

I went home feeling a bit tired, but also excited that I would be able to move out faster than originally planned. I was going to start apartment hunting right after I left the meeting tomorrow. When I pulled up to my mom's house, I saw a shiny new silver BMW parked in front of the house. It looked familiar, but I couldn't pen point where I saw it at. I walked up to the door and turned the lock. My jaw nearly dropped when I saw Lauren sitting in the living room with a woman and my mother.

"Misha come in." My mother waved me over. She knew I would be pissed, but what my mother didn't know is that I was also capable of homicide.

"Why is she here?" I asked with the look of death.

"Honey, listen before you go off." My mother stood up and walked toward me. Lauren looked in her hands careful not to look me in the eyes. The woman stood up and faced me.

"Hello, I'm Lauren's mother Diane." She extended her hand, but I only looked at it with disgust.

"So you're the woman who birthed this home wrecking, trifling, disloyal tri." My mother cut me off before I could finish my sentence.

"Misha Joyce Carter. I know I've raised you better than that."

I let my mom pull me by the hand into the living room. To say I was confused as to why this trick was here was a huge understatement. I had to give it to her she had more balls than a little bit.

"I don't have anyone else to go to Misha," Lauren claimed.

"Don't talk to me, don't' say two words to me or I swear," I threatened.

"Misha, I'm not really sure why you're upset with her, but may I talk to you instead?" Diane interrupted. I turned my attention on the stranger.

"Lauren's father is looking for me to do bodily harm. Lauren was asking your mother if it would be ok for me to stay here for a few days until we can figure something else out," Diane continued. I heard what she was saying, but nothing was registering. I couldn't believe this bitch thought she could still come to me after what she's done. If my mother wasn't there, I would have ripped her head clean off her shoulders.

"It's the only place he won't think to look." My mother chimed in. I turned to look at her in disbelief. I believed in God, but if she wanted me to go along with this she was going to have to show me the exact scripture that said I should help before I agreed.

I pulled away from my mother and walked over to Lauren. She jumped up from the couch to prepare for what she thought was coming.

"I want to talk to you alone. If you don't jump at me, I won't jump at you." I spoke through gritted teeth. I needed answers that Tori couldn't give me.

"Misha, we don't have time for that. He's looking for her now." My mother spoke from the background.

"If you make me decide now, my answer is hell no and to hell with them all," I answered without taking my eyes off of Lauren. She looked scared, but tried to keep her brave face on. It was time for her to make up her mind. I wasn't going to make it up for her unless she did something stupid. She gave me a head nod that said yes she agreed. I turned to walk up the stairs.

"It'll be ok mom." I eased my mom's fears. I could tell she was nervous.

Desperate Times Calls for Desperate Measures
Lauren

I knew my dad wasn't going to stop looking for my mom until she was six feet under. While I was at her house he sent me another message saying he knew I lied about the hotel incident but he wasn't upset because he found out how dirty Shannon really was. He ended his message telling me that he had someone on the job as far as my mom went. My mom brought the crazy out in him, which scared me. I needed her to be safe and I knew that my dad would be trying to track her, but the only place I knew she'd be safe was at Misha's mom's house. I knew the idea was crazy, but I needed to move fast before he got out of the hospital. I was willing to do anything to keep my mom safe even if it meant begging Misha's mom to have mercy. I knew she was into the church so I prayed she had mercy on me.

I made my mom pack up a few things and told her to put them in my car. I tried to explain the situation between me and Misha, but I couldn't bring myself to tell her my part. When we got there Misha's rental wasn't there so I thought I would have a better chance talking to her mom alone. Just as I expected she was willing to listen until Misha came in. My heart nearly dropped to the floor when I saw her. She had venom in her eyes so I lowered mine. If I were her I would probably kick my ass and send me on my way. When she said she wanted to speak to me alone I knew what she wanted and I knew that would be the only way I could possible get her help. I followed her upstairs to her bedroom. I looked around and remembered how many nights I spent the night there just a few years ago.

Misha closed the door behind us and told me to sit on the bed as she sat on her desk chair. Her eyes had daggers and I could tell her heart was racing.

"You have a lot of damn nerve coming here thinking I would give a damn about any problems you have." She crossed her arms in front of her.

"This is the only place I know she'd be safe," I interjected.

"I don't give a damn."

"Listen Misha, I know I'm lower than dirt in your eyes right now, but this is urgent." I wanted to make her understand that this was a matter of life and death.

"Tell me why? Why did you do it? You see I know why Tori did it, but for the life of me I can't figure out why your spoiled ass had to go there." Her words cut deep. "I'm waiting," she antagonized.

"Because I fuck with men who don't give a damn about their wives, and I saw how much Tori loved you and how you didn't appreciate him. I didn't set out to fuck him, ok? After it happened, I felt guilty as shit. But the reality is I got to feel how you should have felt. Happy to have a dude who wanted you for you. Tori didn't complain or talk shit about you. He never once said you ain't do shit for him. You told me that. I wish I could take it back, but I can't. Misha you have a mom and I finally found mine and my dad wants to kill her because of something he did years ago. You don't have to like me. You don't have to ever talk to me again, but I can't lose her twice." I started crying. I felt like an ass for coming here. I stood up to walk to the door.

"Sit down!" Misha yelled. I backed up and sat on the bed again.

"You're right I don't like you anymore, I will never talk to you again, and if my mom wants her to stay there is really nothing I can do to stop her. But it's ok cause I'm leaving," she said before standing up and walking back downstairs. I didn't know what to say. I just stood up and followed.

Misha stood in the living room and told her mom.

"This is your house, so I can't tell you what to do. I'm only going to say that I'm sorry Ms. Diane that you weren't around to raise your daughter in a way that wasn't as reckless as she is. On that note mama, I'm going to be moving out soon." With that she grabbed her purse and headed out the door. Misha's brother walked in at the same time.

"Jerry, please help Ms. Diane grab her bag." Misha's mom instructed her youngest son.

"Who?" he asked looking confused. He rolled his eyes in my direction before walking back out. I followed him to my car and pointed at the suitcase in the back seat. He grabbed it and walked it in the house. My mom was standing on the porch.

"I'm going to call you, please don't leave the house without letting me know first. I'm going to go talk to Chris to see about getting you security. I'm sorry for putting you in this situation." I got in my car and drove toward the club. I hit Chris's number on my cell.

"Hey!" he answered on the second ring.

"Hey Chris, how's everything?" I asked about the club.

"Everything is going ok, they should be done by the middle of next week. So we might be able to open up next weekend." He sounded happy about that. I wished I could be just as happy.

"Good, are you still there? I have a few things I need to run by you," I asked.

"Yeah, I'm here, where you at?" he asked.

"On my way, meet me in the back office. I'll be there in a few minutes," I said before disconnecting the call. I was there in less than ten minutes. I locked the car doors with the key and knocked twice on the heavy metal door.

Chris opened the door to let me in. He looked real good in a tight fitting black muscle shirt and a pair of jeans. He pulled me in for a hug like he read my mind.

"Thanks," I said when he was done.

"What's up? What you need?" he asked from over his shoulder.

"There are some things I'm going to tell you. You don't have to get involved if you don't want." He sat in the chair in front of my desk and gave me the 'what could this be about?' look.

I told him about what my dad did to my mom and the events that just took place. I let him know that I needed his help protecting my mom, but would understand if he chose not to get involved.

"Come on Lauren, you know I got you no matter what. Let me make a few phone calls and I'll get that handled," he answered.

"I don't want them to hurt my dad I just need her protected until I can figure out what we need to do. I have her in a safe place. Let your friend know money isn't an issue." I spoke more nervous than I should have been. I didn't know all of what Chris was capable of. I decided that I would need to confront my father again to see what he planned on doing.

I sent my dad a text and told him I was coming to the hospital. He responded with a smiley face and the name of the hospital.

"Oh yeah, Tori stopped by earlier looking for you," Chris said. I looked up from my text surprised.

"Really? Did he say for what?" I asked trying to contain my excitement.

"Naw, I really didn't sit and listen though," Chris replied honestly.

"Thanks." I wasn't sure if I should be happy or if I should ignore it. He did just play the hell out of me over at his house. I wondered what he wanted though. I thought about Misha and what she was doing for my mom and thought I needed to make sure she was safe before I did anything stupid.

I spent another thirty minutes at the club before telling Chris I needed to go. He walked me over to the door.

"Look Lauren, I'm here if you need me, ok babe?" he asked before leaning in and kissing me softly on the lips. Without realizing it I closed my eyes and returned the kiss. His lips melted into mind and his arm reached around my waist, drawing me closer. I let my lips explore his, gently licking his bottom lip. He made me feel safe in that moment like he really could take care of me, protect me from anything. I just prayed I didn't need to use his protection any time soon.

When he finished kissing me I could feel him getting hard on my leg. It made me smile.

"Thanks Chris, I needed that. Now go take care of your business, just don't do it in my office." I looked down at his manhood, smiling before turning to walk to my car. I drove toward the hospital with a smile on my face. Chris has managed to lift my spirits with that one simple kiss. I parked in the hospital parking lot and felt a bit of dejavu. I was directed to my father's room and walked in hesitantly.

"Dad?" I asked to see if he was awake. He turned around slowly, his face expressed pain.

"Lauren, I'm glad you came." He smiled, but I was furious looking at him.

"Dad, you went to that hotel room to kill my mom." I stated matter of factly.

"Lauren, I need you to try to understand something," he started, but I was already done with him.

"Why didn't you tell me that you have a brother?" I asked with my arms folded.

"Because you didn't need to know." He spoke like a no nonsense dad for the first time in forever.

"How can you say I didn't need to know I had extended family?" I asked incredulously.

"I am your only family. I don't need to explain that to you. Whatever Diane told you is a lie." He looked away and off into space like he was thinking up ways to make her pay.

"I'm an adult and you don't have to protect me anymore. I'm old enough to know the truth," I said it, but felt like a little girl at the same time.

"Do you know why I never had more kids?" he asked.

"No," I whispered back at him.

"Because I didn't want them to live in your shadow. You are a star Lauren and its hard living in the shadows of a star. I didn't want another person to feel like they weren't good enough because of how brightly your star shines. You didn't need to know about my brother because I was tired of living in his shadows." My dad started and I tried to follow. It was hard though, knowing who he really was. "I was tired of living in his shadow and I didn't mean to hurt your mom, but I wanted him to pay. I wasn't thinking straight. I'm not sorry about it though because I had you."

Laughs Last
Tori

I picked a hole in the wall bar and told the bartender to keep my tab open. I ordered two coronas and guzzled them down before taking a second breath. With a wave of my hand the bartender passed me another two. After sitting there for another ten minutes, I felt someone sit to my right. Glancing over I noticed a pretty, well dressed black woman with curly black hair and noticeable red lips.

"I'm sorry," she said thinking she must have bumped me.

"You're fine." I went back to drinking my beer.

"Long day?" she asked with a pleasant smile on her face.

"Well, if you call having your wife walk out on you in the middle of marriage counseling a long day, then yes I guess I am." I spilled my life story with no inhibitions.

"Ouch, sorry to hear that." She made a face.

"It's fine. I tried my best and that's all I could have hoped for. You live and you learn," I remarked not really feeling like having a conversation.

"Very true. I'm Veronica." She turned in my direction, extended her hand for me to shake, and smiled broadly.

"Nice to meet you." I shook her hand and stood up with my beer and walked to a quiet table. I wasn't in the mood for a conversation or even picking up any women. I wanted to wallow in my misery alone in silence. I could hear the beauty suck her teeth as I walked away. I'd apologize later if she was still there when I was ready to leave. I sat with my back against the wall and watched the other people drinking away their problems.

An older man with silver hair caught my attention. He looked sadder than the typical men there. I watched as he took out what looked to be a picture from his wallet. He stared at it for a long time while he drank. Once his beer was gone he tucked it neatly back into his wallet and stood up to leave. I imagined that would be me, sitting sad thinking about my life and all I lost. I knew there were plenty of women out here for a brother like me to choose from but I really wanted Misha. What hurt me the most was knowing that she could have probably forgiven me if it wasn't with Lauren. *'Was it worth it?'* I asked myself, and the answer was no.

The one thing I wasn't going to do was sit around acting like a damn fool if she wanted to walk away. I loved her, but that would kill me. A waiter came to my table with a shot glass full of Hennessey.

"The lady over there sent this to you." He pointed in the direction of the bar, Veronica was there turning to smile at me. I took the glass and drowned it before placing it back on the tray.

"Tell her I said thanks and sorry for walking off," I told the waiter who left to relay my message. I watched him give the woman my message. She nodded in my direction. Moments later she stood and walked toward the bathroom near the back of the bar. My eyes followed the sway of her hips. She turned slowly and used her hands to coax me over. I pointed an index finger to my chest and mouthed the word, me? She nodded a yes, I stood quickly, not allowing myself to think about my actions. I walked over to Veronica noticing how much shorter she was to me.

We didn't talk, she pulled me into the unisex restroom and locked the door. Her lips pressed hard against mine as I grabbed her waist to lift her to the sink. Her hands roamed my back and pulled on my shoulders. Her brown skin smelled sweet like caramel body spray. I wanted to devour her. I felt her fingers reaching for my belt. I pulled back just enough for her to unfasten it. The lady killer was hard as a brick wall as I grabbed a handful of her breast. She moaned in my ear and wrapped her legs around my waist.

"Please give it to me." She breathed into my neck. I was sure I was going to deliver on that request. I pulled her shirt out of her skirt and let my fingers find their way to her hard nipples. My fingers massaged them hard. She winced with pain, but I didn't care. I wasn't in a love making mood so she would pay for my anger, frustration, and disgust with myself at having ruined what I had.

I pulled her off the sink and pushed her shoulders down until she dropped to her knees. I rubbed my swollen dick on her face, looking down at her with a bit of unrestrained rage. She used her hand to push it away. I didn't relent, but forced it near her mouth where I held her by her hair to keep her steady.

She started pushing my hips back.
"Move, move now!" she shouted. I moved back a little and she scurried to her feet and ran out of the bathroom adjusting her clothes. I just stood there with my manhood in my hands, staring at my reflection in the mirror above

the sink. I had officially hit rock bottom. I fixed my clothes and went back to the bar to pay my tab. I didn't hold eye contact with anyone there, just walked out and got into my car. The drive home felt like forever. Seeing Veronica's face brought me back to reality. I wasn't that dude and I knew it, but I didn't give a damn if she was angry. I walked away from her first and when you mess with an angry man you don't know what you might actually get back. I pulled into my driveway and sat in the car for a few minutes before heading inside.

Most of my night was a blur, I drank the last of my Corona's from the fridge and kicked off my shoes to watch a few games. It wasn't long before they were watching me. The sun hitting my face along with skid marks across a gym floor made me wake up. I slept the night on the couch again. I flicked the remote to turn off the television and ran up the stairs to relieve myself. My watch said it was already seven in the morning. I needed to get myself together for work. I stripped quickly before I jumped in the shower, five minutes later I was in my room finding something to wear. I didn't stop in the kitchen for breakfast just ran out to my car with head pounding. I would need a cup of coffee to calm it down.

I was grateful U.S. 78 wasn't backed up on my way to the office, it wasn't a good look to be late on your first day back. When I arrived my favorite parking spot was free. I slid in and headed into the office making sure I hit the lock button with my keys. A few of my buddies at the office yelled out glad your back. I gave a head nod on my way to my small office. I knew I was backed up so I would need to get a move on. I still needed to leave early enough to make it to my divorce meeting with Misha. Mr. Hartford walked into my office without knocking. He is my dept. manager and overseer of most of my projects.

"Glad to see your back Tori, is everything ok?" he asked concerned.

"Well sir, to be honest my wife and I are getting a divorce. I have to get to a meeting with her lawyers a little later today." I let him in on my problem.

"Very sorry to hear that son. Well if you have to go early that's fine, just stop by to let me know when you leave." He put his head down and walked out of the office. I checked my company emails and my online work folder to see what I missed. Surprisingly, I only had a few layouts to do and one new assignment sent to me this morning.

The meeting with Misha was at three thirty so I would need to leave a few minutes earlier. I stuck my head in Mr. Hartford's office. He was on the phone. I did the 'I'm leaving' sign with my thumb and head motion. He waved me goodbye. Barrett, a tall thin black guy with black rimmed glasses, stood beside me waiting for the elevator.

"Hey man," he spoke first.

"Hey Barrett, how you been man?" I asked.

"Pretty good, can't complain." The elevator pinged and we both stepped on. I always felt awkward around him. He seemed like the kind of guy that was more interested in reading than anything else.

"You know, you never come with any of us for drinks after work. You don't drink?" I asked him curiously. It was something that I always wanted to know.

"Actually I do, but my wife just had a baby and I like to be home to help her out as much as I can." He looked my way. I felt the pang of jealousy creeping into my chest.

"Good for you man," I said instead. I walked off the elevator first when the doors opened. "See you tomorrow." I said over my shoulder.

I was determined not to let this meeting throw me off my game. I didn't care what Misha wanted and I damn sure didn't care what Arnold had to say. I wasn't going with a lawyer because I made up my mind on a few things, but would let them play out at the meeting. I hopped in my car and hit the radio. "Turn Down for What?" was cranking from the speakers. I turned up the volume and nodded my head like I didn't have a damn care in the world, though the world was weighing heavy on my shoulders. I pulled up to Arnold's uppity ass office building, parked in my spot, and walked in through the revolving doors.

"How may I help you?" A beautiful brunette with cherry red lips asked.

"I'm here for Arnold Blake, I have a meeting. I'm Tori Carter," I spoke politely, after all she didn't have anything to do with it.

"You can go to conference room A. down the hall and to your left." She pointed me in the right direction. The place looked expensive with all of the glass structures, A-line design, and uncommon architecture. I walked into the conference, the first to arrive yet again. A few moments later Misha walked in holding her purse. She wore a pair of tight fitting jeans, a white tank top shirt, blue waist length blazer, and a large brown belt. My eyes followed her ass as she walked by.

"Tori," she acknowledged my presence as she took her seat. A young white guy in a suit came in and sat beside her, then Arnold walked in wearing a tailored made business suite.

"No lawyer?" he asked sarcastically.

"I don't need one." I spoke sarcastically. He laughed which provoked my anger. I took a deep breath. I would have the last laugh today though so I would remain cool.

"Well, my client has decided that she would only like you to buy her a car for her to get back and forth to work. She would also like you to agree on a small amount of alimony as well," Arnold started. I looked over at Misha. She studied my face. What she asked for was fair. I didn't have any objections.

"What if I don't a divorce?" I asked making the junior lawyer looked puzzled.

"Well, you both would have to wait a year before she is able to continue, but if you ask me you've already made your choice." Arnold sat down arrogantly. Misha knew what she was doing when she got this bastard to take the case.

"I didn't ask you your opinion," I snapped back.

"Tori, there isn't any need to prolong things. Do you realize that if we stay together I won't be the same woman you married? I will constantly question you and everything you do?" Misha asked.

"You won't have to ask because I will make sure you know. I know what I need to do on my end. I won't let you live in doubt. I'm a man about mine Misha and you know that." I tried to sway her one last time. She looked as if she was thinking it over.

"Misha, you don't have to listen to him. If you're ready for divorce, it's up to you to make that decision," Arnold continued to stoke the fire burning in the pit of my stomach. She turned toward Arnold then back at me before putting her head down.

"I need time apart Tori. I need to clear my head to decide what I need to do for me," her voice cracked. I wasn't giving her time to think anything over. She isn't going to live apart from me and then decide she doesn't want me anymore. It's now or never and that was my final offer.

"Misha, I'm telling you that I will never do anything else to hurt you like I did before. If you live somewhere else while you think it over, we both know what you'll decide. You either want me or you don't. It's now or never," I was growing impatient.

"How dare you give me an ultimatum, Tori! You can't tell me when my heart will heal or how much time I need to think things over. You must be crazy," she snapped. I saw the fire behind her eye that always drove me crazy.

I pushed my seat back and stood up. I didn't have time to continue with this back and forth. I said what I said and I meant it. She was either going to love me or leave me.

"If you don't take my offer now that's fine, but I want you to know that I'm taking the adoption center to court to get my son back. I never gave my consent for him to be adopted and therefore he belongs to me."

Her eyes grew wide and Arnold's head snapped in her direction. I walked toward the door and walked out. If I can't have her, I want what we both created.

Made in the USA
Middletown, DE
05 January 2016